Death Dyed Blonde

Death Dyed Blonde

STANLEY REYNOLDS

QUARTET

First published in 2008 by
Quartet Books Limited
A member of the Namara Group
27 Goodge Street, London W1T 2LD

A catalogue record for this book
is available from the British Library

ISBN   978 0 7043 7135 4

Typeset by Antony Gray
Printed and bound in Great Britain by
T J International Ltd, Padstow, Cornwall

1

First there was the body of the thief. He was hidden in the bushes in Old Compton twenty-five feet from the boat-dock. His throat was slit and there was a knife in the grass alongside him and it might have been suicide except a small-time thief like Billy Zoots was not the suicide type.

A twelve-year-old kid had found the body and he had come across the lake and into the police station at North Holford to tell them.

Davy Shea thought the kid was making it up.

'I know this kid,' he said. 'He's the Wilson kid, he's always causing trouble, Boomer.'

'Give the kid a chance,' said Parker Daniels, the police chief, whom everyone called Boomer.

'A body?' Davy said to the Wilson kid. 'What kind of a body?'

'A dead one,' the kid said, 'with yellow hair. It's Billy Zoots.'

'How do you know it's Billy Zoots?' Parker asked.

Davy answered for the kid. 'The yellow hair,' he said, 'everyone knows Billy Zoots with the yellow hair. Him and his pal Elroy Green got bleached blond hair. It's a pretty stupid thing for a pair of thieves to do, making themselves stand out like, that but they're slaves to fashion, I suppose.' He turned to the kid. 'What were you doing out there?' he asked. 'Were you trying to sneak a look at Julia Naundorff's bulgers?'

A week or so ago Julia Naundorff, the movie actress, had moved into a house in Old Compton on the other side of the lake. Until then no one had known that she owned the house, which was on a farm, but apparently she did.

Since then the town had kept a look-out for her, but no one had seen her. It was said she was going to give up acting and become a recluse.

Davy was still inclined to believe there wasn't a body in the bushes, but it was a good day for a drive, a perfect summer morning in June, and Davy thought maybe they'd get a chance to see the movie star.

He and Parker drove with the kid out to Old Compton to the Naundorff house and there was the body, just like the Wilson kid had described. It was tucked away out of sight in the thick bushes. If the kid hadn't spotted it, the body might have gone unnoticed for weeks.

Billy Zoots was lying on his back. His hair was bleached to a startling yellow. He had a number of rings in his ears and one in his nose and around his throat was a big red necklace.

'This is disgusting,' Parker said, looking at the body. 'I don't know if I really want to keep on doing this.'

Davy looked at the tall, thin police chief standing there in an incredibly wrinkled shirt with a frayed collar and high-water trousers and Davy thought that he was joking and then he saw that he wasn't.

'Well,' Davy said, 'you're not a lawyer any more, Boomer, you're a cop, you've got to see this stuff.'

Parker had been a lawyer. When the mayor made Parker the chief because of trouble in the force people were surprised. Parker hadn't been a very successful lawyer – people thought he was a little crazy – and they didn't think he'd make much of a police chief; but in a small township where nothing much happened they didn't think it would matter.

Parker was standing in the beautiful June morning sunshine staring at Julia Naundorff's house on top of a little rise some two hundred feet from the lake shore and he was thinking there was something strange. No one had appeared. They had come up in a cruiser and they had walked round the boatdock and poked through the bushes and no one had come out of the house to ask what the hell they were doing there.

He turned and glanced out to the big lake, which was thirty miles long. There was a haze over the water but he could see a boat. There were two people in it. They were fishing. He watched them casting. They were too far away for him to see the line but he saw the movement of their arms.

'I wish I was out there fishing,' Parker said.

'This is serious, Boomer,' Davy said. 'This is no time to be making jokes. Maybe the kid killed Zoots. He could have. Kids have done things like that before.'

'What?' the kid said. He started shaking. His lips were trembling.

'Take the kid back to the car,' Parker said, 'and stop giving him a hard time. Jesus, he's only a kid. He'll have nightmares over this. You will, won't you?' he asked the kid.

'What?' the kid said.

'Have nightmares,' Parker said. 'Or do you watch so many horror movies on TV that this doesn't seem like much to you?'

'Are you kidding?' the kid said.

'I don't know,' Parker said and the kid looked at Davy wondering if the tall thin man in the rumpled shirt was all right in the head.

'Call up the coroner's office,' Parker said to Davy, 'get Dr Phyllis Skypeck here.'

'What'll you be doing?' Davy asked.

'I'm going up to the house to get a peek at the movie star's bulgers,' Parker said.

2

Parker walked up the lawn to the big white house. It was a colonial farmhouse and it had been kept in fairly good shape and still managed to look authentic. There was a farm attached to it – on this side of the lake there were several farms.

Parker thought he must have been told that a movie star had bought the house but he had forgotten. As far as he knew, Julia Naundorff had never visited the place. He didn't know who lived there and worked the farm. Julia Naundorff had arrived in North Holford unannounced. Then she was on local TV saying she was going to give up making pictures. She said, like Garbo, all she wanted was to be alone.

Parker had been surprised by the way Julia Naundorff came into town. He had thought a Hollywood star wouldn't go anywhere except with at least a couple of minders, but she had arrived alone.

He got to the house and rang the bell. No one answered. He was walking round to see if he'd have any better luck at the back door when he saw a dust-covered jeep coming up the drive. A woman with her hair tucked up under a baseball cap was driving it. A long pair of suntanned legs stepped down from the jeep and they were so good-looking, despite the old army boots on the end of them, that Parker thought he must be seeing Julia Naundorff. There was yellow hair under the baseball cap. Her eyebrows were blonde too, unlike Billy Zoots she was a real blonde. She was wearing old blue denim shorts and a T-shirt, neither of them perfectly clean, but she had such a splendid figure he didn't think it would matter what she wore.

'What the hell are you doing here?' she said.

She wasn't being very polite and Parker saw that there was something wrong with her mouth. She was wearing lipstick and it didn't go with the farmhand look.

He watched her taking in his frayed collar and the trousers that were too short and not being overly impressed even though she looked like she had been out baling hay or feeding the pigs – except for the red lipstick that looked like a couple of red bees had lighted on her face.

'I'm the police,' he said.

'So?' she said.

'Are you Miss Julia Naundorff?' Parker asked.

'What?' the woman said. 'Are you trying to be funny?'

'I'm sorry,' Parker said, 'I don't go to the pictures, and my TV's broken.'

The woman smiled. 'I'm only the sister,' she said, 'I live here. I've been here ten, twelve years.'

'I'm sorry,' Parker said.

'I'm not. I like it.'

'I meant not knowing who you were.'

'Why should you? I'm just the kid sister. Besides, I've got another last name. I'm Ann West.'

'I don't get over to this side of the lake very often,' Parker said.

'Lucky then that we don't have much crime here,' she said.

Parker frowned. He was going to have to tell her that they had a very serious one now.

Ann West said: 'You're the new police chief the mayor appointed because the other was corrupt. I've heard about you. They call you Boomer. Is that right?'

'That's right,' Parker said.

Ann West smiled and Parker thought again how pretty she was despite the big red mouth.

'There's a dead body in the bushes down by the boat-dock,' he said.

'You're kidding.'

9

She held a hand up, shielding her eyes against the sun as she looked at Parker. She was tall, about five feet ten, but she had to look up at Parker. One eye was closed against the sun. The other eye was long and grey, and he saw now that her eyes were made up with mascara, making the lashes very black. Like the red mouth, it seemed out of place with the rest of her.

'I'm sorry,' Parker said, 'but I'm serious. He's in the bushes and his throat's been cut.'

'I don't believe it,' she said, and she started for the boat-dock, walking very quickly with her stunning figure in the old, worn denim shorts.

'Hold on,' Parker said, 'I don't think you ought to see it.' Parker had to step out to catch up with her.

'Be real,' she said, still walking fast. 'Where?' she said, 'where is it?' Then she saw the body hidden in the bushes. 'Jesus,' she said, 'who is it?'

'Billy Zoots,' Parker said. 'We know him, he's a well-known local thief.'

'Jesus,' she said again, 'I can't look at that.'

She turned away. Parker thought she might faint. He wondered if he should hold her. He stood close to her just in case.

'What was he doing here?' she asked.

'What he usually does, I guess, stealing things or trying to.'

'We haven't had a robbery.'

'Are you sure? You've been out of the house.'

'That's true. I went shopping for some things.' She looked at her wristwatch. 'It's 11.15,' she said, 'Good Lord, I've been away for hours.'

'We'd better go and see,' Parker said.

She didn't look like she was going to faint but Parker stayed close to her.

'Look,' she said, 'I'll go in the house and check it. If anything's been stolen, I'll call you.'

'I'd rather come with you,' Parker said.

She looked up at him as if he were making a strange request. Parker felt himself blushing as those long grey eyes with the black lashes looked at him.

'Is your sister in?' he asked.

'She went out for a drive sometime about 9 o'clock. I went out shortly after. I haven't seen her since.' She took her eyes off him and he felt almost calm again. 'I don't think she's back yet,' she said. 'Listen, can you get that body removed before she gets here? She's highly strung. She's liable to have a fit if she sees something like that.' Her eyes were back looking at him.

'We've called the coroner's office. We've got to wait for the medical examiner to come. Then there are other things we have to do.'

'Christ,' Ann West said, 'Julia will go ape. This is all she needs. She says she's quitting movies and just wants to be quiet, and then a dead body shows up in her bushes.'

She turned and Parker found himself looking at her worn and tight denim shorts. He was glad she couldn't see the way he was looking at her. She went to the jeep and picked up some bags. Parker could see one was full of lemons.

'Let me help you,' he said.

'No,' she said, 'I'll be all right.'

They walked towards the back door.

'That's Julia's car,' she said.

A big BMW with California plates was parked at the far end of the yard almost out of sight, behind a big chestnut tree.

She led him into the kitchen. It was big and disordered in an old-fashioned farmhouse way, also in the way of a woman like Ann West who lived alone and didn't have many people coming to call.

'Julia,' she called out, 'I'm home.'

There was no answer.

There was a phone on a table in the kitchen and the red light was flashing.

'Excuse me,' she said.

She bent over the answerphone and Parker thought again how wonderful she was. He thought he ought to look away, but he didn't.

She pressed a button and a man said his name was H. P. Spendlove. He had a tentative, creepy voice, like he was almost ashamed of himself for having the power of speech. There was something else odd about the voice. It sounded like someone trying to do an English accent and not getting it quite right.

'Miss Naundorff,' the voice said, 'I'm still in North Holford. I went to your house this morning as you instructed, but there was no one there. Perhaps I got the time wrong. Anyway, I'm here. Anytime you want to see me, I'm staying at a place called the College Inn.'

When H. P. Spendlove finished, Ann West said, 'Jesus, that's all we need. He's one of Julia's loonytunes. He believes in reincarnation, but then so does Julia.'

Parker followed her blue denim shorts out of the kitchen.

'Julia!' Ann West called, but she got no reply. 'Where the hell is she?' she said.

The rooms were big and filled with old comfortable furniture. He tried to look at it instead of at her. The edge of a carpet was chewed and the coverings on the lower corners of two sofas were also frayed.

'You've got a terrier,' Parker said.

'Say, you really are a detective.' She managed another smile even with Billy Zoots in the bushes. 'It's a Staffordshire bull terrier, Miss Sheherazade Old Compton Gun Moll. She's not two yet, but she's going to be a champion. I show her. She's got two Firsts in novice bitch. She's black with white socks. Julia's afraid she might catch something off her.'

Parker's eyes followed her glance to a big modern oil-painting on the wall, a portrait of a woman. It didn't go with the old-fashioned room.

12

'That's her,' Ann West said, 'that's Julia. But where's the real thing? Julia!' she shouted. 'Julia! Where are you?'

She stood listening for an answer.

'Jesus,' she said, 'I wonder where she's got to?'

There was no sign of anything stolen downstairs, then as she started to lead him upstairs, his mobile phone rang. It was Davy Shea.

'Boomer,' he said, 'Dr Phyllis Skypeck is here now.'

Parker went back to following Ann West's long brown legs and blue denim backside up the stairs.

He could see right away that there'd been a burglary. The rooms were turned over.

'Oh, Christ,' Ann West said. 'And where's Julia?'

She had been cool after the first shock of seeing Billy Zoots with his throat cut, but she looked again as if she might faint. Parker wished she would. He could catch her.

'This is terrible,' she said. 'This is awful. When did it happen? Who could have been here?'

'Billy Zoots,' Parker said. It seemed obvious, but Ann West had trouble taking it in.

'This is my room,' she said. 'I don't have anything worth taking.'

'Your sister,' Parker said, 'she'd have things worth taking?'

'Oh yes,' Ann West said.

She was shaking now, as bad as the Wilson kid when Davy was going to arrest him for murder. Her red lips weren't trembling, but her hands were. Parker noticed for the first time that she was wearing nail polish. Her finger nails were bright red. That, like her lips, also didn't fit in.

'I'd like to see your sister's room,' he said.

They went down the hallway to what looked like the best bedroom in the house.

Someone had gone through it fairly carefully. The drawers were opened and the contents spilled on the floor. There were a number of expensive suitcases and they were open with the contents spilled on the floor.

Ann West said, 'Julia brought so much luggage with her she hasn't had time yet to unpack.'

She was still trembling and her face was white. She had trouble getting the words out. It was as if she had been running. She was gasping for breath.

'Where the hell is Julia?' she said. 'Burglars, they could get in anywhere, the doors weren't locked. And some of the windows were open. In fact, I think all the windows were open.'

'What's missing?' Parker asked.

'You mean outside of Julia? Jesus, he's taken a Versace dress. I remember seeing it when she hung it up in the closet. And a Fortuny dress too. What's he going to do with things like that? He can't sell them to some girl. They'd be recognised. They're one-off dresses worth thousands.'

'He probably didn't know.'

'He knew enough to steal them,' she said. Her red lips were pressed tight together as she concentrated, with the long grey eyes narrowed, looking about the bedroom to see what was no longer there.

'Jewellery,' she said, 'there's jewellery gone.'

'That'll be easy to trace, I suppose,' Parker said. He imagined a big movie star would have famous jewels.

But Ann West wasn't listening to him. She looked even whiter than before. She sat down on the edge of the bed.

'And where's Julia?' she said. 'What's happened to her?'

They went through the house looking for Julia. She wasn't there.

3

Parker and Ann West came out of the house. The Wilson kid was sitting in the cruiser and down by the lake shore Davy Shea and Dr Phyllis Skypeck were standing in the bushes by the body of Billy Zoots. Out on the lake the morning haze had lifted. The fishermen were still in the rowing boat.

Parker walked down to Davy and Phyllis and Ann West came with him.

'You don't have to come,' he said to her.

'What?' Ann West said. She was still in a daze.

'There's no reason for you to be here,' he said.

'Oh,' she said, and it was as if she hadn't taken in what he said.

The burglary had affected her more than Billy Zoots with his throat cut, but, Parker thought, the dead man was in the bushes two hundred feet from the house, and the burglary was in the house and more personal.

When they came up to Davy and Phyllis, Parker could see Davy taking in Ann West's good looks, wondering if this was Julia Naundorff and then seeing that it wasn't. Unlike Parker, Davy went to the pictures.

Davy's mobile phone rang.

'Hello, Georgie,' Davy said, 'how's things going?'

He stood in the June sunshine listening to Georgie Stover and evidently what Stover was telling him was amusing because Davy was smiling and nodding his head.

Ann West watched Davy too, and her face was still white, but not so white as before. She had stopped trembling. She was beginning to look healthy again, like she did when she came up the drive in the dust-covered jeep and Parker had seen the long sun-tanned legs stepping down as she came to ask him what the hell he was doing there.

Davy said, 'This is a good one, Boomer. Julia Naundorff was seen in her car stopped in traffic outside Gleason's Liquor Mart at 9.30 this morning.'

'What's going on?' Ann West said, but Davy didn't answer her. He spoke to Parker.

'A funny thing happened,' Davy said, 'it's amusing. A guy was trying to rob Gleason's and Julia Naundorff drove up and the guy stopped concentrating on the robbery and stared out the window at her. Ken Gleason thought the guy might go outside and ask for her autograph. Or demand it, he was armed.'

'That's fairly amusing,' Parker said.

'That's not the best,' Davy said. 'When he came into Gleason's he was wearing a mask and he was pretending to be a Puerto Rican. He was speaking Spanish to Ken, but then he saw Julia Naundorff and he got so excited he forgot the Spanish. He started talking American. Georgie Stover was driving by in the cruiser and he saw a masked man in the window and Georgie went in and the masked man just stood there looking at the movie queen. He was also soaking wet. He went into Gleason's to rob the place soaking wet.'

Phyllis Skypeck came out of the bushes. Seeing a man with his throat cut hadn't bothered her.

'Do you have a time of death?' he asked her.

'Not long ago,' she said. 'I'll be able to tell later.'

'What the hell's going on now?' Davy said.

There was the unexpected sound of children's voices. Three little girls were running down the lawn. They were wearing bathing suits and carrying towels.

'Get them out of here,' Parker said. 'They shouldn't see this.'

'The body's in the bushes,' Davy said. 'They won't see.'

'Christ,' Ann West said, 'I forgot about them. They're

16

Whitey Gotton's nieces. I invited them up for a swim this morning.'

Parker could see Whitey Gotton strolling down the lawn behind the running girls. Whitey owned a fishing-tackle place in Old Compton, but before that he had been a big-league ballplayer. Whitey was in his forties and his ball-playing days were over. He hadn't had a long career. He was a pitcher and had had two twenty-game seasons with the Sox and then he was sold to Los Angeles and he had burned up the league until his arm suddenly went. He had taken up fishing to get the strength back in his arm and he had won a couple of casting championships, but the pitching arm never came back. Whitey was a good-looking guy and he never seemed bitter about his days in the Majors getting cut short.

'Whitey,' Davy called to him. 'How you doing, Whitey?'

'Pretty good,' Whitey said. 'I'm feeling pretty good.'

Davy seemed to have forgotten about Billy Zoots. There were always a bunch of men like Davy hanging round Whitey's store listening to Whitey talk about the Majors. It was hero worship.

'Listen, Whitey,' Parker said, walking up to the ball-player. 'These kids. They shouldn't be here. There's been an incident.'

'What?' Whitey said.

The girls ran down the lawn to the boatdock and laid their towels down and stood on the edge of the dock ready to jump in. One of them, the oldest, a blonde girl of ten, went in, but the other two, one eight and the other six, stood testing the water with their toes. Then one of them began to scream.

'What is it, Isobel?' the girl in the water asked the eight - year-old who was the one screaming.

Ann West ran to them on the boatdock.

Isobel kept screaming. The six-year-old stood next to her. She wasn't screaming, she was staring down into the water with her mouth wide open.

Then the girl in the water cried out.

Parker could see her face had an expression on it as if something very disgusting was in the water with her.

Ann West reached down and pulled the girl out and they both stood looking down into the water. Isobel had stopped screaming, but she held onto Ann West. The youngest girl still stood with her mouth open.

Parker came to the boatdock. 'What is it?' he asked.

And then he saw the face of the dead woman in the water.

4

'There's no mistaking who that is,' Davy said.

But Parker didn't know.

'It's Julia Naundorff,' Davy told him.

The dead woman was on the dock now. She was in a two-piece bathing suit, with her blonde hair spread out on the dock's canvas covering. Her grey eyes stared up at Parker as they had when he first saw her face in the water.

'She must have come back for a swim,' Ann West said. 'She went for a drive in town and she came back for a swim.'

She spoke in a mechanical way, looking down at her sister as if she couldn't believe what she was seeing.

'She went for a swim,' Davy said, 'with Billy Zoots dead in the bushes with his throat cut?'

'From the boatdock she couldn't see Billy Zoots dead in the bushes,' Parker said.

He turned to Phyllis. 'Is it a drowning?' he asked. It didn't look like anything else, but he thought he should ask.

'I won't know for sure until later,' the medical examiner said.

Parker saw Ann West look at Phyllis. It was as if she were only just noticing her. Dr Skypeck was young, only twenty-seven, small and slim and pretty, with dark hair and an odd little cat's mouth, with no lipstick.

Parker turned back to the dead woman. Her hair was very blonde – yellow hair, like the kid said about Billy Zoots, and her eyebrows looked like black patent-leather. They made her hair look even more startling. Her hands were long and slim and had bright red polish on the fingernails. She was tall like her sister, and even dead and stretched out on the canvas-covered boatdock Parker could see that Julia Naundorff had been a beauty. 'It's a crime,' Davy said.

He meant a beautiful woman like Julia Naundorff being taken from the world.

'Those fisherman out there,' Parker said, 'they might have seen something.'

There was a motorboat at the dock. Parker took it out to the fishermen, watching the men trying to cast. They weren't very good, but one was better than the other. When Parker drew closer he cut the engine and shouted to the men and they looked annoyed at being disturbed.

'What is it?' one of them, a short, fat middle-aged man, said. He was the one who didn't cast very well, still he was more annoyed about being interrupted than the other, who was younger and taller and slimmer and looked a bit more at home outdoors.

'I'm the police,' Parker said.

'The police?' the fat man said. 'What the hell's this? We breaking a law? What's going on?'

'Let him talk, Sal,' the younger one said.

'I'll let him talk,' Sal said. 'Go ahead and talk,' he said to Parker.

'There's been an incident,' Parker said.

'An incident?' the fat man said. 'What do you mean?'

'A woman's drowned. I wondered if you've seen anything. Over there.' He pointed back to the boatdock.

19

'We haven't seen a thing,' the fat man said. 'Especially not any fish.'

'I saw something,' the young one said.

'What'd you see?' the fat man said. 'You didn't see anything. We don't want to get involved in incidents.'

'We can't talk here,' Parker said. 'Follow me into the shore.'

'I don't know about that,' the fat man said.

'We'll have to do what he says, Sal,' the younger man said.

When Parker got back to the boatdock Julia Naundorff's body was covered up and was being taken away. Davy and Ann West were still there, but Whitey Gotton and his three nieces had left.

Parker stood on the dock and waited for the fishermen. He had to help Sal up out of the boat. The fat man made a comic routine out of it. The younger man sat in the boat smiling like an audience that has seen the comic's turn many times before.

'Hey,' the fat man said looking at the ambulancemen taking Julia Naundorff away, 'what's that?'

'That's the woman who drowned,' Parker said.

'Jeez,' the fat man said, 'that's the incident, huh?' He assumed a sorrowful expression. Parker thought the fat man must be someone who worked in a profession where it was necessary to produce quick changes of emotions.

'Now,' Parker said to the younger man, 'what did you see?'

'Not very much. I only happened to glance over towards the dock. There was such a haze I couldn't see clearly. But I saw a woman in a bathing suit standing on the edge of the dock – and then she fell into the water.'

'You mean she dived in? Or jumped?' Parker said.

'No,' the man said, 'not exactly. She sort of fell.'

'You didn't think that was odd?' Davy said. 'You didn't think that maybe she was in trouble?'

'Not really,' the man said. 'I just thought it was an odd way to go in the water. Then I thought I had a bite on my line and I forgot about her.'

'You didn't look towards the dock again?' Parker asked. 'You didn't see her in the water?'

'No,' the man said, 'if I'd seen her in trouble in the water I would have helped.'

'Naturally he would,' Sal said. 'Naturally Jack and I, seeing someone in trouble in the water, would have gone to help. That's only natural. But Jack didn't see.'

'Maybe she had a heart attack,' Davy said to Parker.

'I didn't see anything,' Jack said again.

He seemed genuinely sorry that he had failed to investigate the woman who had fallen into the water.

'Don't blame yourself, Jack,' Sal said to him. 'She was wearing a bathing suit and she suddenly went into the water, what could be more natural?'

He turned and looked at the bushes. 'Say, what the hell's in there?' he asked.

'Another body,' Davy said. 'Not a drowned one, a body with its throat cut.'

'Jeez,' the fat man said, 'what's going on here?'

'We don't know,' Parker said. 'We're trying to find out. You didn't happen to see anything going on in the bushes?'

'We didn't see nothing,' the fat man said.

'Your friend saw the woman go into the water,' Parker said. 'What time was that?'

'He don't know,' the fat man said.

'Can't he talk for himself?' Davy said.

'Sure he can talk for himself,' the fat man said. 'You tell him, Jack.'

'I don't know what time it was. I was fishing.'

'That's right,' the fat man said. 'Time don't mean a thing to Jack when he's fishing. To me time hangs very heavy and goes real slow when I'm fishing.' The fat man looked about as though trying to find another topic of conversation.

'That's a nice house,' he said, 'a real nice place.'

'It's Julia Naundorff's,' Davy said, 'or it was hers.'

'What?' the fat man said. 'What's that you said?'

'The movie actress,' Davy said, 'Julia Naundorff, that's her body going into the ambulance. She's the woman who went into the lake.'

'Jesus,' the fat man said, 'that's who we came to see. Julia Naundorff, she's why Jack and I are here. We're in the picture business. We wanted to talk her out of retiring.'

Parker took a statement from them and let them go back fishing, and they went off in their boat.

5

The scene-of-crime squad arrived. The North Holford township police didn't have the manpower and Parker had to send for the State Troopers at Great Plimpton to get the scientific people who find footprints and fingerprints. But the weather was hot and dry and there were no footprints outside.

'This knife,' the scene-of-crime woman said, 'it didn't kill him.'

'It must have been his own,' Davy said. 'He probably took it out to defend himself.'

'Well,' the woman, a redhead, said, 'he wasn't quick enough. There's no blood on it, not his and not anyone else's.'

When they finished outside, they went into the house where there were only the fuzzy marks left by the thief's gloves. Parker thought he could have told the redhead that and saved her the trouble, but, he thought, it must be a reassuring sight for people seeing the scene-of-crime woman at work. She had an expensive-looking black leather case with strange instruments inside. She even had magnifying glasses like Sherlock Holmes and she wore thin, white rubber gloves that gave the impression of a surgeon involved in a delicate operation.

Parker and Davy watched the redhead working for a while and then they grew bored by all that science and went down to the kitchen. Ann West was there. She sat at the big table in the kitchen looking sad.

A man came into the kitchen. He was carrying a black and white dog.

'Ann,' he said, 'I don't mind looking after Moll when you're out, but my wife, she's nervous of dogs.'

'Has she been trouble?' Ann West said. She took the pup from him.

'No, but my wife is frightened,' the man said. Then he said, 'Hello, Boomer, Davy' and went out as if it didn't surprise him seeing two cops there.

Ann West put the pup on the floor.

'We'll have to get a complete list of what was stolen,' Davy said to Parker. 'That's the way things are done.'

Parker saw Ann West looking at him, possibly wondering why he had to be told such basic things. Then she turned her golden blonde head away and went back to looking vacant and sad. Parker wondered how she had managed to live here on the lake for ten or twelve years without him ever seeing her. He thought that if he had seen her even once in that time he would have remembered.

Suddenly she turned to him and said, 'I've got things to do. This is a farm. I've got animals to see to. They can't wait no matter who gets drowned.'

'We've got to have a list of what's been taken,' Parker said.

'Yes,' she said, 'I heard him tell you that.'

Parker felt himself going red. 'I know,' he said, 'I'm not a real policeman. I'm an invention of the mayor's. I have to rely on real cops like Davy.'

Ann West said, 'And has he told you why none of the things that were stolen were found by Billy Zoots' body?'

She was being sarcastic. Parker felt himself going red again. Ann West smiled.

'Billy Zoots,' Davy said, 'he never worked alone. He wasn't much of a thief. He was a look-out and he wasn't much of a look-out. He was too well-known. In fact, a man who hired Billy to be his look-out really wouldn't know what he was doing, but that description fits Elroy Green who worked with Zoots.'

Ann West wasn't looking vacant any more. She didn't even look particularly sad.

'So,' she said, 'you might find out who did it?'

'I think probably so,' Davy said. 'A small-time place like North Holford township gets small-time thieves. The thief who came here, he'd be out of his league stealing big-time designer clothes and expensive jewellery. He won't know what to do when he comes to sell them.'

'That could be ages from now,' Ann West said. 'And what if it wasn't some local yokel thief? What if it was someone big-time from out of town?'

'There's Billy Zoots,' Davy said. 'Somebody from out of town wouldn't hire Billy Zoots. I guess when we pick up Elroy Green, we'll have the man who killed Zoots.'

'This is all very interesting,' Ann West said. 'I'm having a hell of a day, but I've got those animals to see to. Can I go now?'

She looked at Parker when she said this, paying him the respect of pretending that he was in charge.

'Sure thing,' Parker said.

Ann West smiled at him again. Parker supposed it was another kindness because he looked such a dummy and out of his league.

She said, 'You'll let me know what's happening, won't you? If something comes up, you'll let me know?'

Parker said he would.

Ann West picked up the Staffordshire bull terrier pup and left to do her farmwork, Parker and Davy went out to the cruiser where the Wilson kid was still waiting and drove away from the house down the drive that was full of potholes.

'Some place for a movie star to end up,' Davy said.

Parker had been thinking the same thing.

'It's almost,' Davy said, 'as if she were planning to hide out from someone here. Well, with her gone and drowned we'll never know the story now. We'll never know why she decided to come running to a backwoods farm after the high life like she was used to leading.'

'You think she was on the run?' Parker said.

'Well, she was trying to escape those Hollywood guys. They told us that themselves.'

The Hollywood guys were the two fisherman. Parker had taken their statements and let them go back fishing. They were staying at the Lake House Hotel on the other side of the lake. The short fat one was Julia Naundorff's agent and the young one was a writer who had, the short fat one kept saying, a script that Julia Naundorff couldn't refuse. The writer, whose name was Jack Coolidge, said he was going to stay and do some more fishing, but the agent, who was called Sally Sallas, wasn't keen. Still, he said he would stick around until Julia Naundorff's funeral. She had been one of his biggest stars, he said, and then he asked Parker when he thought the funeral would be, as if he wanted her buried then and there so he could be off.

Davy drove through Old Compton, which wasn't as pleasant as its name. There was good farming land around it, but the main street was deserted and the stores looked run-down, with their business having gone to the big supermarkets just off the freeway. Whitey Gotton's tackle shop came into view, with Whitey standing outside talking to a group of men and boys.

'Whitey's all right,' Davy said, 'he's a great guy.'

'Is he?' Parker said.

'Sure he is,' Davy said, 'what's wrong with Whitey?'

Parker didn't know, except Whitey Gotton had a sort of swagger that Parker found objectionable. He couldn't tell Davy that, Davy also had an objectionable swagger.

They dropped the Wilson kid off at his house and then drove round the lake to Brown's Ferry and waited some time for the car ferry to come and take them across. It was crowded with tourists. They had already heard that a big Hollywood star had drowned in the lake that morning, but they weren't sure which movie star it was. There was no talk of Billy Zoots being murdered.

When Parker and Davy came off the ferry, they drove to North Holford to the little police station in the main street and young Georgie Stover was there looking excited because he had arrested the guy who tried to rob Gleason's Liquor Mart.

'Wait until you see him. You won't believe it,' Georgie said.

6

The stick-up man was a good-looking guy called Spa Johnson, an obvious character, behaving as if he wasn't in real life in a real police cell, but was an actor playing a part.

'That was a fine scene, was that a wrap?' he asked, as if they had been filming a movie.

'I think he's crazy,' Georgie said. 'He could have got away, but he just stayed in Gleason's waiting for me to come in and arrest him.'

Spa's shoes were wet. He was creating marks on the floor.

'Stand still,' Davy said, 'stop roaming around messing the floor.'

'It was hot,' Spa said, 'I got myself under a hose on a lawn. Under a sprinkler system on the lawn of one of those fine houses on Freemount Street.'

'You'll be cooling off plenty in a cell,' Davy said.

'Don't be ridiculous,' Spa said. 'Where's my team of lawyers? I've got a battery of high-priced attorneys-at-law who are going to get me walking out of here a free man in the morning.'

'You're not very good at this,' Parker said. 'Why don't you try something else?'

'Not any good!' Spa said. 'My Spanish was perfect. It was the Hollywood star. I couldn't believe it, seeing a Hollywood star. I got carried away. I love the movies. I'm going to be an actor. When I get my break, that's what I'm going to be.'

'Why didn't you run away when Georgie arrived?' Parker asked.

'I was still thinking of Julia Naundorff,' Spa said. 'I was mesmerised by that Hollywood star. You see her in *Postman's Knock*?'

'No,' Parker said.

'You get yourself a DVD and see her in *Postman's Knock*,' Spa said, 'she was great.'

'She's dead,' Davy said.

'Who? Julia Naundorff? You're spoofing.'

Davy told him. Spa looked crushed. He was obviously a fan.

'I can't believe it,' he said, 'but she'll live for ever on the silver screen.'

Davy said, 'I'll tell you who else is dead. Billy Zoots, you know him? He's dead too, with his throat cut.'

'Billy Zoots?' Spa said. 'You're joshing. Who'd want to kill Billy?'

'He was helping rob Julia Naundorff's house,' Davy said, 'and he got his throat cut. Who'd Billy Zoots be robbing a house with, except Elroy Green? Do you know where Elroy is hiding out these days?'

'How'd I know? I don't rob houses. I don't even rob liquor stores.'

'Listen,' Parker said, 'we don't want to ruin a guy like you. We don't want to put you away. We don't even want to have you in court. I can get Ken Gleason to forget about it, if you could help us with this Billy Zoots business.'

'Billy Zoots,' Spa said, 'dead? I can't believe it. And Julia Naundorff? It's hard to believe.'

'Nevertheless, it's true,' Parker said.

'Elroy,' Spa said, 'maybe he had something to do with it. He's a big talker. He says he can go steal on order anything you want. You want, say, Brooks Brothers' shirts, Elroy will go and steal them for you. He don't steal nothing but top-class items. You give him your size, Elroy will get them for you. At least he says. Or he was saying, to Billy Zoots. Can I go now?'

'Not yet,' Parker said. 'Where's Elroy now?' he asked Davy.

'I don't know,' Davy said. 'I can't keep up with all of them, and they keep changing their names. Do you know, Georgie?'

Georgie Stover said he couldn't remember where Elroy was.

'Now listen, Spa,' Parker said, 'you try and find out where Elroy is and you walk out of here a free man.'

'What the hell is this, Boomer?' Davy said. 'You can't let him go. We've got to make an arrest. He's a gunman.'

'Have you seen the gun?' Parker said. 'He wasn't going to shoot anyone with that gun.'

Davy looked at the gun. It was a replica.

'Still, what the hell?' Davy said. 'He's a robber.'

'Not any kind of a serious one,' Parker said. 'We send him up to the state pen, he might get real good and serious at it.'

'Jesus, Boomer,' Davy said, 'you're not a defence lawyer now, you're supposed to be a cop. We haven't got time for sociology.'

Parker ignored Davy. He said to Spa, 'You think hard about Elroy. You try to come up with an address and I'll see you're all right.'

'And when you get this Elroy, you going to let him go too?' Davy asked, but again Parker paid no attention to Davy.

It was lunchtime and Parker went to the phone and called Ann West.

'Listen,' he said, 'we've got someone who might know who robbed your place. At least he might know where the fellow is who could have been working with Billy Zoots. Chances are whoever was working with Billy Zoots had a falling out with him and killed him. I'd like to get that list of stolen things now, if it isn't too much trouble. When we go to Elroy Green's house, it'd be best if we know what was stolen. Could you write some description of the Versace dress and the Fortuny one? I wouldn't know what they are supposed to look like.'

When he put down the phone he said to the others, 'Ann West is making a list for me. I'll go out to Old Compton to collect it.'

'She's a good-looking woman,' Davy said, 'not as beautiful as the sister, but still. Is she your type, Boomer?'

'I don't have a type,' Parker said.

'Sure you do,' Davy said, 'everyone has a type.'

'I'd hate to see yours,' Spa said.

'I heard that,' Davy said.

'Did you?' Spa said. 'It always surprises me someone like you having the power to comprehend human speech.'

'You going to let him get away with this, Boomer?' Davy said.

'Down at the zoo,' Spa said, 'they'd make a fortune with you in a cage, making the folks pay to come in and listen to an animal like you with the power of speech. I look at you and I hear you talking and I am amazed.'

'You're going back to the cell,' Davy said. 'He's begging for it.'

'Leave him alone,' Parker said. Then he said to Spa, 'You'd better watch out. If you get Mr Shea angry, he's going to shoot you. Mr Shea hasn't shot anyone in ages and he's getting anxious.'

'Is he going to walk?' Davy said. 'You can't let him walk, Boomer.'

But Parker was already out the door.

7

When he got to the farmhouse in Old Compton, he thought Ann looked different. She wasn't in mourning, she wasn't wearing black, she was still in the worn blue denim shorts and the dirty T-shirt, but she had taken off the lipstick, mascara and nail polish. That, he thought, might be a form of mourning.

He went into the kitchen and the Staffordshire bull terrier was there. She jumped at Parker.

'Moll,' Ann said, 'get down.'

'She's all right,' Parker said. He patted the dog.

'I see you like dogs. Have you got one?' She pulled the little bitch away from Parker.

'I had a Norwich terrier, but she died,' Parker said.

Ann made a sad face. 'You ought to get another dog,' she said.

'I'd be worried I couldn't spend enough time with it.'

'You don't have a wife and family?'

'I had a wife and two kids, two girls, but I'm divorced, a long time ago now. The girls are in Boston with their mother.'

Parker hoped he wasn't sounding like a victim. When he met a new woman and was forced to tell her about his marital state, the woman always asked if he saw his daughters and it was painful when he had to say that he hardly saw them at all now, but that when his wife first ran away, the girls had lived with him for four years. Fortunately Parker met very few new women, so he didn't have to tell them the painful story. He didn't think Ann qualified as one of them. She was strictly police business; except she was so good-looking, even better now that the

31

lipstick and paint had been removed. If he had a type, Ann West would be it, Parker thought; and then he caught sight of himself in a reflection in the glass door of a kitchen cabinet and he thought the tall goofy-looking man in a frayed shirt would not be any woman's type, at least not as her first choice. It made him feel ridiculous about criticising Ann's lipstick and fingernail polish.

'I've never been married,' Ann said. 'Sometimes I've thought about it, to get another pair of hands on the farm. But it's too big a price to pay.' She smiled to show this was merely a comic remark.

'Was your sister going to help on the farm?'

'Are you kidding?' She looked at Parker. 'I guess you weren't fooling when you said you'd never seen Julia in a movie. A lot of men, when they first met Julia, would try to pretend that they didn't know who she was. I suppose they wanted to give the impression they liked her for her own sweet self, not knowing she was a famous movie actress. She never fell for it, she never fell for anything.'

Parker wondered if Ann had disliked her sister. He saw her looking at him and he guessed she knew what he was thinking.

'I hardly ever saw her,' she said. 'We're not really sisters. Her mother married my father and Julia came with the marriage. That was in Pennsylvania. My own mother was dead.'

Parker could feel himself pulling a sad face like Sal the fat fisherman had done. He felt a complete phoney doing it, but he thought it was polite.

'Then Julia's mother, Kim, ran off. I guess I'll be getting a call from Kim. I guess that now Julia's dead, Kim will be coming around to get her hands on the money. She'll be in for a surprise.'

'Oh?' Parker said.

He wasn't interested, but he thought he shouldn't show it; and, besides, it gave him the opportunity to look at Ann

West without seeming rude.

'H. P. Spendlove,' Ann said, 'the man who was on the answerphone?'

Parker nodded. He remembered the name.

'He's getting the money,' Ann said. 'Isn't that a joke? Julia was keen on reincarnation. She's already given Mr H. P. Spendlove a fortune for his research, now he's going to get some more.'

Parker wondered if Ann was bitter. He decided she wasn't. She, in fact, sounded pleased about it, as if it were a joke on her stepmother. She smiled to make sure he got the joke.

'I hope Kim comes to the funeral,' she said. 'It'll be wonderful seeing her face when Mr H. P. Spendlove gets the money.'

'Your sister was really going to retire to Old Compton?' Parker asked.

'She said so.' Ann paused. 'Oh,' she said, 'I see what you mean. Yes, I could have done with her here and her money helping out. The farm isn't doing that well. The truth is, I did run into trouble a while back and Julia helped out. She gave me the money I needed. You could say she owned the house and the farm. There, I've told you that. I'm ashamed of it. I don't tell people. Why should I? But I guess you've got an honest face. Or you're the kind of cop that wheedles things out of people.'

Parker thought he was getting too interested in Ann West, or, at least, that it might start showing, which, he thought, would be embarrassing.

'The list,' he said, 'of stolen things?'

'Here it is,' she said. She got up and went across the kitchen. Parker watched her long legs. A farm girl, he decided, was the best sort of woman to meet if you were living in the country. Other women, even if they were born here, had longings for life beyond the horizon.

Ann came back across the room and Parker pretended to

be looking at something else. There was a Staffordshire bull terrier calendar on the wall he pretended he was looking at.

'Here's the list,' she said. 'I've tried to describe the jewellery and the Versace and Fortuny dresses, so you'll recognise them, but I'm not too good at that sort of thing.'

Parker's mobile phone rang. It was Davy.

'Spa Johnson,' Davy said, 'he's remembered, Elroy Green lives at 89 Liberty Street, in Elmwood.'

'I'll come back,' Parker said, 'and go with you. I know 89 Liberty Street.'

'And Spa?' Davy said.

'Let him go. I'll speak to Ken Gleason.'

'Jesus, Boomer,' Davy said, 'I hope you know what you're doing. The mayor picked you to fight the corruption in the force, not to let prisoners go.'

Davy was one of the cops Parker had been warned about when the mayor made him the chief. He was said to be occasionally on the take, but so far Parker hadn't caught Davy on the take.

When he finished talking to Davy, Parker said to Ann, 'We think we know who robbed you.'

'Oh?' She seemed only vaguely interested.

'Someone called Elroy Green from Liberty Street, in Elmwood. I'm going there now.'

'Well,' she said, 'you've got the shopping list. I've got work to do.'

She walked ahead of him down the hallway to the front door.

'Do you think he did it?' she asked.

'What?' Parker said.

'Killed Billy Zoots? Did this Elroy Green do that?'

34

8

'Who else would have done it?' Davy asked.

They were in the North Holford station getting ready to go to Liberty Street to pick up Elroy Green for at least questioning. The phone in the station rang.

'It's never stopped,' Davy said. 'It's the media, and also just people, wanting to know about Julia Naundorff.'

'And Billy Zoots?' Parker asked.

'They don't care about Billy Zoots,' Davy said.

'Why should they?' Spa said. 'Julia Naundorff was a star. Billy Zoots is just another dead thief.'

'What's he still doing here?' Parker said about Spa.

'I thought you'd change your mind,' Davy said. He turned to Spa. 'Get back in the cell,' he said. 'Boomer, you shouldn't allow prisoners to walk around here like they were at home. What if the mayor strolls in? Or one of the selectmen?'

'You can go,' Parker said to Spa.

'You sure?' Spa said. 'I don't mind staying.'

'See,' Davy said, 'he wants to stay. He knows the law.'

'Better than you, fatso,' Spa said to Davy. 'Everybody knows all about you, with your hand in the till.'

'I'll kill him,' Davy said. 'Lock him up, Boomer, or I'll kill him.'

'You better get out of here,' Parker said to Spa.

Still he seemed reluctant to go, but finally he left with his wet shoes making marks on the floor.

Parker and Davy left the station. The town centre looked good, with the grass on the village green still a deep colour. By August, it would be faded and turned brown in places. The bandstand on the green had been recently painted and sparkled in the sun, and the old white-painted colonial church and the College Inn, also painted white, looked better than they did on the too-brightly coloured postcards that tourists bought.

'Bob Blanchard will be making money if people come to Julia Naundorff's funeral,' Davy said. Bob Blanchard was the owner of the College Inn. 'I suppose,' Davy said, 'Ann West will be doing all right now with Julia Naundorff's money coming to her. That farm, it looked a trifle run-down.'

'She's leaving her money to some reincarnation fellow,' Parker said.

'Is that right?' Davy said. 'I'd heard about her believing in that, but I thought it was just a newspaper story.'

'You're a fan?' Parker said. 'You read about the movie stars?'

'I read the papers,' Davy said, 'I'm not like you, reading only books. Of course I'm not a former big-time Boston lawyer.' This was sarcasm. When Parker was married, he had lived in Back Bay, Boston and worked in his wife's father's law firm in State Street. It had been a giant step up for Parker because he was only a night-school lawyer when he met the Boston attorney's daughter. When his wife ran away, Parker could have stayed in the firm, but it was embarrassing and so he came back to North Holford, but he hadn't been successful. People thought it was because he had the two girls to look after, but when the girls went back to live with their mother, people saw that Parker was still unsuccessful. Then they said it was because he was crazy, or at least a clown. He was glad when the mayor made him the police chief. He needed the money. People now said they couldn't see what the mayor was playing at.

'It's a shame she isn't going to get the money,' Davy said of Ann West as they drove to Elmwood in the cruiser. 'That'd be a good woman for you, a looker, on a farm, with

36

some money, some really big movie star money, you'd be all right again.'

Parker's wife had been rich. That was what that 'again' meant.

Parker was going to tell Davy to shut up about his prospects for romance, when Georgie Stover called and said there was trouble at Hadley Falls, a domestic, with a woman killed.

It was out of their way, but Parker said they'd go. Davy drove fast but they were a long time getting to Hadley Falls and when they arrived at the house, there didn't seem to be any trouble.

'No one called no one about nothing,' the woman said.

'That's right,' the man said.

They were an old couple sitting on their front porch and the woman hadn't a mark on her, except for what time had done.

'Someone's been wasting police time,' Davy said when they left the old couple still sitting on their porch. 'It's kids. The old folks must have annoyed them some way.'

When they finally got to Elmwood it was another place, like Old Compton, that sounded better than it was. People in North Holford township liked to pretend that the only run-down slum property was six miles away in the city of Holford, which was a disused milltown and looked it, but North Holford township also had its slums, and Elmwood was the chief among them. Liberty Street was full of old wooden houses that needed paint.

Street scenes slipped past the car window. Any number of children briefly played on cracked concrete sidewalks. An out-sized woman in summer undress floated by like a badly inflated balloon. A row of tough faces on a street corner glanced at the cruiser, then disappeared.

'A zoo,' Davy said.

Behind the summer street scene, rickety wooden tenements, two and three-family houses, tilted over brief ragged lawns, the houses separated by barely an arm's reach.

'Christ, what a dump,' Davy said. Then he became embarrassed, remembering that Parker came from Elmwood. 'I supposed it's changed a lot,' he said.

'No it hasn't,' Parker said.

The cruiser pulled up at the address in Liberty Street.

Elroy Green did not advertise his presence among the names over the six bells at the front door. One card was new, bigger than the others – it said that a Miss Maria Esperanza did readings.

Davy rang the ground-floor bell, waited only a short time and then with the flat of his hand rang them all at once, then stooped and shouted through the letter slot 'Open up, police.'

'The Ritters had a candy store here,' Parker said. 'That was years ago.'

A woman's face appeared at an open upstairs window.

'You,' the woman said, 'what do you want? Miss Maria Esperanza isn't here. This is the second time today I had to tell someone that.'

Then she saw the cruiser parked at the kerb and the rather unmistakable cop's face on Davy.

'Oh,' she said, 'you don't want Miss Maria Esperanza.'

'No,' Davy said. 'We want Elroy Green.'

'That figures,' the woman said. 'I'll be right down. It's open anyway. It's broke, at least most of the time.'

Davy tried the door. It didn't open.

'See,' the woman said and then her face disappeared.

There was the sound of shuffling feet and then the front door opened.

The woman said, 'Someone came for Maria Esperanza earlier and I thought you were more come to see her. She's often busy, even at this time of day. But she isn't in.'

'That's very interesting,' Davy said, 'but we've come for Elroy Green.'

'You,' the woman said to Parker. 'I know you. You're Boomer Daniels. You're still tall.'

Parker bent his head and took in the woman. It was incredible. It was old Mrs Ritter. But that was impossible. She was dead.

'I'm Estelle,' the woman said, 'Estelle Ritter, you won't remember me, Boomer, you were so tall. I remember you coming into the store and you've kept getting taller.'

'Estelle?' Parker said.

'That's right. I closed the store. Six, seven, eight years ago, it got too much for my legs, and on account of the robberies.'

She was an exact copy of old Mrs Ritter. Parker tried not to look at her too closely, in case she read his mind. Old Mrs Ritter had wispy hair, she had been bald in patches and she often wore a wig. Estelle's hair was also wispy now.

'I know what you're thinking, Boomer,' Estelle said, 'you're thinking I'm the spit of ma. You were a kid then, Boomer, we were all kids, you thought ma was old. She wasn't old. She was only sixty, but the kids thought that was ancient. I'm past ancient now.'

'This is all very interesting,' Davy said again, 'but where's Elroy Green?'

'He ain't here,' Estelle said. 'I told you that. I knocked on his door to ask him something, but he's not here.'

'We better check,' Davy said.

'You don't believe me?' Estelle said.

'We have to check,' Davy said.

They went into the house.

'His room's on this ground floor,' Estelle said. 'In the back. I thought of moving to the ground floor once, on account of my legs, but it's not safe with the break-ins, and plus we always lived upstairs, you remember, Boomer?'

'Yes, I do,' Parker said. 'You used to have good times.'

'That was ma,' Estelle said, 'always singing. Dad wasn't so much fun.'

As they went down the hall, a woman appeared on the stairs. She was blonde, good-looking, with a dark Hispanic complexion.

'Miss Esperanza,' Estelle said, 'I didn't think you were in. You had a caller.'

'A caller?' Maria Esperanza said. 'I didn't have any appointments today.'

'A woman,' Estelle said. 'She rang the bell and I shouted down, "Who is it?" and she said "Esperanza". I let her in to wait for you.'

'I haven't seen anyone,' Maria Esperanza said.

'Maybe she changed her mind,' Estelle said. 'She looked to me like a woman who got smacked by her husband. She was a big blonde, wearing sunglasses. Maybe she decided she didn't want to learn if she'd get smacked any more in the future and went back home.'

'I'm going out for a reading now,' Maria Esperanza said. 'I just thought I'd tell you, I saw someone out in the back earlier.'

'Another thief?' Estelle said.

'Maybe so,' Maria Esperanza said. 'I saw him and then I looked again and he wasn't there. There was something strange about him.'

'What was that?' Estelle asked.

'I don't know what it was,' Maria Esperanza said, 'something not right.'

She came further down the stairs and stepped into the sunlight that was coming through a window and her hair looked very blonde, like Billy Zoots' or Julia Naundorff's.

'I hope it wasn't another thief,' Estelle said. 'You cops, you ought to do something about these break-ins.'

Maria Esperanza went past them. Parker watched Davy looking at her retreating figure. She was good-looking. Parker watched her himself.

'She does the readings,' Estelle said. 'She used to be very big at it, in Boston, only something happened and she left.'

When they got to Elroy Green's door, Davy knocked, but there was no answer.

'I told you,' Estelle said. 'He's out. I knocked twice already. On account of the rent.'

'You got a key,' Davy said. 'Open it.'

'Without a warrant?' Estelle said.

'That's right,' Davy said.

Estelle unlocked the door and pushed it open.

'Oh my gawd,' she said.

'Jesus,' Davy said.

Elroy Green with his amazing bleached blond hair was there, dead with a cord round his neck.

9

'What the hell's going on here?' Davy said. Have we got some sort of crazy serial killer who hates bleached blonde hair?'

'I was wondering that myself,' Parker said. 'Julia Naundorff had blonde hair too.'

'But she wasn't murdered,' Davy said.

'Maybe not,' Parker said, 'but something made her fall in the water.'

'Well, Dr Skypeck will find out all about that,' Davy said.

They went back to examine Elroy Green's room.

It had been turned over. Parker saw a dress on the floor that looked like the Fortuny dress that Ann had described for him.

There was one open window in the room, it was wide open and looked out on the back yard. A fire escape ran up to the top floors.

'Anyone could easily climb in here,' Davy said.

'That man Maria Esperanza saw?' Estelle said.

'Or,' Parker said, 'the woman who came to see Maria Esperanza. She never saw Maria Esperanza and you didn't see her leave. Maybe she went out the back after she killed Elroy.'

'It was a man Maria Esperanza saw,' Estelle said.

'Look at this place,' Davy said, 'it's like a stockroom.'

The room was filled with stolen items. There was a pile of brand-new men's shirts.

'Elroy, he was a dresser,' Estelle said.

'These are all different sizes,' Davy said. 'Spa Johnson was right. Elroy stole to order. Look at this stuff.'

As well as the shirts, still in their cellophane packages, there were cashmere and lambswool sweaters in a range of sizes and colours.

'He was in business,' Davy said. 'He was an entrepreneur. You could do with some new shirts, Boomer. How about I turn my back and you make a selection? And there's a jacket that'd fit me.'

'You sure you didn't hear anyone breaking in?' Parker asked Estelle.

'Not a thing. I was upstairs with my legs, except when I came down to knock at his door.'

'Were there drugs here? Did Elroy Green sell drugs?' Davy said.

'I wouldn't know,' Estelle said. 'He paid his rent. At least he did until the last two weeks.'

'Well,' Parker said, 'Elroy is the one who was at Julia Naundorff's. There's the French dress, but where's the jewellery?'

Davy was on the other side of the room poking around.

'Is this it?' he said.

Parker went over and looked at the jewellery Davy had found.

'Some of it, at least,' he said, 'but where's the rest of it?'

He wondered if it was in Davy's pocket. He took out the list Ann West had made and checked the pieces.

'Well,' Parker said, 'we've found these at least, and some-one stole the other dress, the Versace one. Do you suppose Elroy got an order for a Versace dress, and has sold it already?'

Parker was standing by Elroy Green's body. He didn't want to look down. Then he did. The cord had cut into Elroy Green's neck and there was blood.

'We'll have to get a photographer and that fingerprint redhead,' Davy said. 'And the medical examiner.'

Parker was still carefully not looking at Elroy Green. He was looking out the window at the overgrown garden that led to the alley that ran behind the houses in Liberty Street. There were grape vines. He remembered reaching up and picking grapes as he came down the alley when he was a kid.

'Jesus,' Davy said still standing over Elroy Green, 'look at his face. Look at those eyes.'

'Death, it's hardly ever nice,' Estelle said, 'and I suppose murder never is.'

10

Parker was in the station trying to look at the photographs of Elroy Green.

'That's a fancy knot,' Spa Johnson said about the way the cord was tied round Elroy's neck. 'Why should anyone go to that much trouble knotting a rope?'

'What are you still doing here?' Parker said.

'I went away, but then I came back,' Spa said. 'I'm interested in detection.'

'Why don't you go home?' Davy said to him. 'We don't do free rooms here for the criminal classes, unless we are going to charge them with something.'

'The criminal classes?' Spa said. 'That's good.'

'Get out of here,' Davy said, but Spa didn't move.

'Why did he leave the cord?' Parker asked. 'Why didn't he take it with him? After he strangled Elroy Green, he should have taken the cord. Instead he tied it round Elroy's neck.'

'There's blood on it,' Davy said. 'He didn't want to take something with the dead man's blood on it. It could be traced.'

'I don't suppose this cord could be traced,' Parker said.

'I shouldn't think so,' Davy said. 'You can get that type of cord everywhere.'

'But you can't get that fancy knot everywhere,' Spa said.

'The woman who came to see Maria Esperanza,' Parker said, 'maybe she saw something.'

'Maybe she'll come forward,' Davy said, 'but I doubt it. She won't want to get involved.'

'What if she did it?' Parker said.

'She'd have to be a very strong lady,' Davy said. 'Green was almost decapitated. Besides, the door was locked.'

'Maybe she knocked and he opened it for her,' Parker said.

He glanced at the photographs. They were almost worse than being in the room with the body. That didn't make sense, but in the room Parker was distracted by other things. At least he could look at other things.

'The man who Maria Esperanza saw outside,' Parker said, 'I wonder if she could give a description of him? Of course he was some distance away and she only looked briefly.'

'Maybe she could hypnotise herself and remember him,' Davy said.

'Does she do hypnotism?' Parker said. 'I thought she only did readings.'

'I was making a joke,' Davy said.

'Oh,' Parker said, and he looked at the knot that Spa had called fancy.

The telephone rang.

'It's for you,' Georgie Stover said to Parker. 'It's Doc Skypeck.'

Parker took the phone.

'Boomer,' Phyllis Skypeck said, 'I've got something you should see.'

'Something about Elroy Green?'

'No. About Julia Naundorff.'

'What is it?'

'It's better if you see for yourself.'

'Where are you? At the morgue?'

'Of course I'm at the morgue.'

Parker put down the phone.

'Listen,' he said to Spa, 'you want to play detective? Go around your pals, find out if anyone's got jewellery to sell.'

'Me?' Spa said. 'I don't have friends in the criminal classes.'

'It'd be very expensive jewellery,' Parker said. 'Out of the ordinary.'

'I'm no police informer,' Spa said, 'I can't do a job like that.'

45

'He's right,' Davy said, 'this is police business, it should be handled by police.'

'That's right,' Spa said, 'so the cops can find the jewels and pocket them for themselves.'

'What the hell do you mean by that?' Davy said.

'I guess the meaning is clear,' Spa said.

'Here's a list of the jewellery stolen from Julia Naundorff,' Parker said.

He handed Spa a copy of the list Ann had written. The items they had recovered at Liberty Street were crossed out.

'This is big time stuff,' Spa said, looking at the list. 'Nobody I know would have anything like this.'

'He more than likely doesn't know how good it is,' Parker said. 'That's what I'm counting on.'

'Is this dangerous?' Spa asked.

'Two men have been murdered,' Davy said. 'What do you think?'

'I think,' Spa said, 'that this isn't playing a Puerto Rican gunman with a toy gun.'

'Listen,' Parker said, 'if you don't want to do it . . . '

'What about Ken Gleason?' Spa said.

'Forget that,' Parker said, 'I don't want to strong-arm you.'

'I'll do it,' Spa said.

'Do you have a job?' Parker said.

'Do I look like a man employed?'

'I'll get you a job,' Parker said. 'You like play-acting, I'll get you a job at the Lakeside Players.'

'The summer stock theatre? Playing what?'

'Playing moving the scenery,' Parker said.

'And manning a broom?'

'Of course pushing a broom,' Parker said. 'Maybe you'll be discovered.'

'What the hell's this, Boomer?' Davy said. 'Have you gone completely nuts? What will the mayor think, you letting criminals go and getting them jobs?'

'He'll think he made a big mistake making me the police chief, then he'll hope nobody else finds out.'

'Jesus, Boomer,' Davy said, 'you don't care.'

'I'm only an invented policeman. I'm play-acting like Spa.'

He left the station to go see what Dr Skypeck had discovered.

11

The dead body of Julia Naundorff was on a table. There was a sheet covering all but her head and shoulders and Parker was glad about that in case Phyllis Skypeck had opened her up.

Julia Naundorff's face was very white. The blonde hair looked startlingly yellow and unreal, like a bad wig.

'What I want to show you is this,' Phyllis said.

She pointed to a mark on the dead woman's right temple. It was faint, but when Parker bent down to get a closer look, he saw it quite clearly. It was about an inch and a half long and narrow.

'What is it?' Parker asked.

'She was hit by something. I don't know what. There's no residue. It's been washed clean in the water.'

'Maybe she hit her head on something when she went in the water?'

'I don't think so.' Phyllis was gazing at the mark. 'I'd like to open her up and see how much damage it did. You see, she didn't die from drowning. She was already dead when she entered the water.'

'A heart attack?'

'Maybe. Or maybe something else.'

'Poison?'

'That could be, but there's this mark.'

'When was she killed, if she was killed?'

'I don't know for sure. She was in the water. Maybe I'll be able to tell by her stomach content. If a woman like this ever bothered to eat anything.'

'Spa Johnson saw her outside Gleason's Liquor Mart at 9.30. She wasn't dead then.'

'I suppose that's true enough,' Phyllis said. 'You'd better go now, Boomer. Unless you want to watch.'

Parker didn't want to watch.

He went back to the station. When he told Davy what Phyllis Skypeck was doing, Davy whistled. Davy wasn't usually impressed. In a small place like North Holford township, there weren't usually crimes big enough to impress anyone, but he was impressed now.

'That'll be something,' he said. 'Jesus, that'll put us on the map, a movie star murdered.'

'It's impossible,' Parker said. 'The fisherman saw her fall into the water. He didn't see anyone hit her. Of course, he could be lying.'

Davy said, 'If we think the phone's ringing now, it'll be nothing compared to what's going to happen. We're going to look like a bunch of hicks if we can't find who did it. You better start praying Dr Phyllis Skypeck comes up with zip on that head wound.'

'Where's Spa?' Parker asked.

'He's gone out detecting,' Davy said. 'You'll see him around town in a trenchcoat and snap-brim hat any minute now. Jesus, that's going to look good, you letting a guy like that, a criminal, do your legwork.'

Parker remembered he hadn't eaten all day. He wasn't hungry, but he thought he'd better try to eat. He left the station and wandered down the street to the Puritan Maid Diner, but the lunchtime specials were off the menu and it was too early for the hot suppers. He had a coffee and a piece of pie and thought that there was going to be a whole mess of trouble if it turned out that Julia Naundorff hadn't fallen into the water and drowned.

He was having a second coffee when a solemn-looking man came in and sat down next to him at the counter.

'Boomer,' he said, 'how you doing?'

Parker didn't recognise him.

'You don't remember me,' the man said, 'we were at high school together. I didn't have a beard then.'

The man had a short beard and a moustache. He looked respectable, in a coat and tie. He had the look of a native son who had come home all dressed up to show how well he was doing elsewhere.

'I've been out of town for some time,' the man said. 'I'm teaching now in Boston, at BU.'

'Edgar Johnson?' Parker said.

'That's right. I'm glad I've run into you, Boomer, I want to thank you for what you've done for my brother.'

'Your brother?'

'Yeah, my brother Bob. He was in a spot of trouble, you gave him a break. That was good of you.'

'I'm sorry,' Parker said, 'I can't remember.'

'It only happened today,' the college professor said.

'Spa Johnson is your brother?' It didn't seem right to Parker. Edgar Johnson's father had been a doctor. Spa Johnson didn't act like a doctor's son.

'That's right, he's my brother. He calls himself Spa now. He's still behaving like a kid, but he's twenty-five. His trouble is he's too good-looking, all the women go for him, they make things too easy. What the hell he was playing at down Gleason's Liquor Mart, I don't know.'

'I guess he wasn't serious,' Parker said.

'It sounds like serious trouble to me,' Edgar Johnson said, 'not like when he was a kid, taking off from school to go fishing and stealing things from stores. He ought to be grown-up now.'

'Maybe he'll mature,' Parker said.

49

'I hope so,' Edgar said, 'but I just wanted to thank you for what you did. I hope you don't get in trouble for it.'

When Edgar Johnson left, Parker had another coffee and thought about the trouble he might get in for letting Spa off. It had been a crazy thing to do, but if Spa learned anything about the deaths of Billy Zoots and Elroy Green, it would be worthwhile. In the meantime, there was the death of Julia Naundorff to worry about.

Parker decided that Phyllis Skypeck was being overly enthusiastic in her search for a sinister cause for Julia Naundorff's death. She was a drowning victim. The movie actress had drowned. They had a number of drownings at the lake. People went swimming or out in a boat and they got careless and they drowned. There was nothing very unusual about it.

He sat on at the counter until the dinner specials came on the menu, but he didn't eat, he had another coffee instead. The light was already faded when he left the Puritan Maid and walked back to the station. There, he sat staring at the photos of Elroy Green, glad that he had missed dinner as well as lunch.

The telephone rang. Georgie Stover answered. The call was for Parker.

'Yes?' Parker said, trying to keep cheerful.

It was Phyllis Skypeck.

'Boomer,' she said, 'do you want me to give you the science, or should I just tell you?'

'Just tell me.'

'OK,' she said, 'I'll give you the science later. It was the blow on Julia Naundorff's head that killed her.'

12

Parker drove to Ann West's house in Old Compton. As he came up the dusty drive to the house, he saw a tractor pulling a tedder across a field of cut hay. The machine stopped and Ann, in a baseball cap and a baggy shirt, jumped down and came across the field to him.

'Hello,' she said.

She removed the cap and her blonde hair fell loose. Yellow hair, Parker thought, using the term the Wilson kid had used about Billy Zoots. But Ann West's yellow hair was beautiful. Parker couldn't recall ever having been so moved by a woman's hair. She stood with a hand held up, shielding her grey eyes against the sun. The grey eyes were beautiful too.

She saw the way Parker was looking at her. She glanced down at her clothes.

'We're hay-making,' she said. 'We're terribly late this year because of the rain. The barley is almost ready and we haven't made hay yet.'

She turned and looked back to the field where a baler was slowly moving up a line of piled hay.

'It's good weather now,' she said, 'it'll be good hay, but it's still late, and the earlier you make it, the sweeter it is.'

The hayfields ran down to the lake, as did the pasture where she grazed her animals. It was a slightly incongruous sight, Parker thought, the fields with farm machinery and men working, then the grazing cows and sheep, and then the lake full of boats and people playing. The sound of voices shouting from the lake were sharp against the noise of the labouring farm machines. It was sad to think that Ann West would make a small fortune if she abandoned the hard work of farming and sold the house and land to a property developer, who'd rip it down and dig it up and turn it into another tourist attraction.

But Ann West's house was already a tourist attraction. A speedboat came close to Ann's boatdock and slowed. There were teenagers in it. One of them pointed to the house and the boatdock where Julia Naundorff had died, then the boat speeded up and went off, leaving a long, curving wake. The wash from the speedboat smacked the bushes on the shore where Billy Zoots had been found. The bushes were thick, making Parker think once again that it was only chance that got Billy Zoots discovered so soon after the murder.

'I'm afraid,' he said, 'that I have some unfortunate news.'

'Oh?' Ann said.

He felt he should have a sad expression on his face that would convey to her how much he was concerned about her troubles but he didn't think he could manage it when he had so much pleasure looking at her.

'Would you like some lemonade?' she asked. 'I've made some. I've been out in the fields all morning thinking about lemonade.'

'I'm sorry,' Parker said.

'Are you? Why?'

'For keeping you from your lemonade.'

'Come into the house,' she said. 'You can tell me your news then. Have you found out some more about the boy in the bushes?'

'No,' Parker said as he walked along beside her towards the house, 'it's your sister. She didn't drown.'

He thought it would be easier to tell her now, instead of sitting opposite her at the kitchen table. This way, she would not be looking directly at him, seeing how incompetent he was with even second-hand sorrow.

'What do you mean?' she asked. She didn't sound

alarmed. She seemed only slightly curious. 'Did she have a heart attack or something? I know so little about her. She was practically a stranger. I wouldn't know if she had been in bad health. If she was, she never said.'

They were at the screen door leading to the kitchen. The door was old and needed paint and the wire screening was buckled. Parker thought how homey it was. The whole house was like that, far removed, he thought, from the sort of place a movie star would want to retire to. He imagined Julia Naundorff living by a swimming pool, with palm trees under a sky full of perpetual sunlight that was something like a neon sign. He could not see her here, in this kitchen, with the sound of farm machines droning in the background and bees buzzing at the windows.

'She died from a blow to the head,' he said and then he told her what Phyllis Skypeck had told him.

Parker could hear his voice sounding dramatic, as if the scientific words that Phyllis Skypeck had given as the cause of Julia Naundorff's death had a special meaning, something like poetry written in an obscure style that would force the reader to turn to a dictionary. In a courtroom before a jury, a prosecuting attorney would try to make them sound strange, as if the human body, the skull of a man or woman, was a fragile and complicated thing and that a hideous crime, much more cruel and calculated than a simple blow to the head, had been committed.

'You mean someone killed her,' Ann said, 'that it wasn't an accident?'

'It looks that way,' Parker said.

He had to glance at her. She seemed annoyed or puzzled by the news.

'But the man saw her fall,' she said. 'He didn't see anyone hit her.'

She turned her blonde head, looking across the kitchen to an open window where a bee had come in and was attempting to pass through the glass of a pane and could not understand what had happened to the sky, that it had suddenly turned solid.

'You weren't here?' Parker said.

'What?' she said, turning back to him. 'Oh, I see, I'm a suspect, of course. But I wasn't here. I was in town, shopping.'

'People saw you in town?'

Parker tried to sound kind. She must have realised this because she smiled.

'Yes,' she said, 'I can tell you where I was and give you the names of the people who saw me.'

She began to tell him.

'Just a minute,' Parker said, 'I'll have to write this down.'

When she finished, he said, 'That clears that up.'

'Yes, once you've talked to all those people and seen that I'm not lying. But how could Julia have been hit on the head, the man saw her going into the water?'

'It's a mystery,' Parker said. 'And who killed Billy Zoots? He was killed at the same time.'

'Oh yes, I'd forgotten about that.' Her face became sad, thinking about the young thief, dead in the bushes. 'I can't believe it,' she said. 'Any of it.'

The grey eyes were looking at him. Her mouth moved to say something, but she obviously thought better of it. Parker kept looking at the blonde hair.

'The lemonade,' she said, 'here I am, learning that my stepsister was maybe murdered and all I can think of is how thirsty I am.'

She went to the refrigerator, took out a big pitcher of lemonade and poured out two glasses. It was home-made, from real lemons.

'I haven't had this in years,' Parker said.

'I've got to bring some to the men in the fields,' she said. Then she said, 'Is it murder? Can't it be something else?'

'Like an accident?' Parker said. 'I suppose it could be

some sort of bizarre accident, like something falling from an airplane, but somehow I don't think so.'

'But who'd want to kill Julia? And up here, in this place, she didn't know anyone here.'

'We've found one of those dresses and some of the jewellery,' Parker said.

'You have? Where?'

'A local thief called Elroy Green had it. We found it in his room in Liberty Street in Elmwood.'

'That's good,' she said.

'The trouble is,' Parker said, 'we also found Elroy Green – dead. He'd been strangled. We'll want you to take a look at the dress and the jewellery to make sure they're your sister's.'

'Of course,' she said.

'Later on you'll get it back. We'll have to hold on to it for a while.'

'It would be no use to me.' She paused for a moment. 'This is terrible,' she said. 'Three murders.'

'When we learned that Billy Zoots worked with Elroy Green, we thought Green must have killed him after some falling out over the robbery. But then finding Elroy Green dead complicates matters, and the other dress and some of the jewellery are still missing. A woman saw someone in Elroy Green's backyard.'

'A woman?' Ann seemed distracted.

'A Miss Maria Esperanza. She's a clairvoyant. She does readings. She lives in a room above Elroy Green's, in the house on Liberty Street. Maybe she'll be able to come up with a description.'

'Those men,' Ann said, 'the Hollywood ones in the boat, the man who said he saw Julia fall into the water, and the short fat one, Julia's agent, they're probably the only two people in North Holford township who knew her.' Then she said, 'About the jewellery, maybe I made a mistake, do you want me to check?'

'If you wouldn't mind.'

She put the pitcher back in the refrigerator and he followed her down the cool hallway and upstairs to Julia Naundorff's bedroom, which was hot and stuffy with the windows closed.

'I'm not very good about jewellery,' she said. 'That was Julia's thing. I only remember it because she made a point of showing me. The necklace was new. She wanted me to see it, and then she got out her other stuff. It was odd because she must have known I wasn't interested.'

Parker watched her going methodically through her sister's things. She had an efficient way of working, the economical habit of someone who was busy all day long.

'No,' she said, 'it's not here.'

She was standing some feet away from him and Parker watched her yellow hair moving as she looked around the room. He tried not to look at her.

'You'll come down to the station later on?' he said. 'To look at the jewellery – and the dress?'

'Sure. I don't mind. But I'm very busy today.'

'The hay?'

'Yes. It's a very nervous time of year, hay-making, watching the sky for a little cloud in case it's going to rain.'

They went downstairs and into the kitchen. She took the pitcher of lemonade out of the refrigerator. The bee had managed to find the opening in the window. Ann walked Parker to his car.

'Thanks for the lemonade,' he said.

'The Hollywood men in the boat,' she said, 'they said they were fishing. Do you think they're telling the truth?'

'It's an awful big coincidence, them being there when she went into the water,' Parker said, 'and that other man, H. P. Spendlove. He was here that morning. I hope you still have the tape of him on the answerphone.'

She said she had.

'I think I'd better take it with me,' Parker said, 'now that it's something more than a simple drowning.'

Ann put the pitcher of lemonade down and went back into the house. She returned with the tape.

'Do you know H. P. Spendlove?' Parker asked.

'No,' she said. 'I didn't know anyone of Julia's.'

Parker put the tape in his pocket.

'He sounds a mystery man,' he said.

He got into his car and turned round in the drive. In the rearview mirror, he could see her blonde hair swinging as she carried the pitcher of lemonade out to the men in the field. She looked like a woman without a care in the world.

13

The stores Ann said she had gone to the morning her stepsister had been killed were close by in Old Compton.

A grocer remembered seeing the movie star herself drive by in her German car with the California plates at 9 o'clock and then a quarter of an hour later Ann had come in to buy lemons.

'She was driving that old jeep of hers and she parked right outside,' he said. 'I remember her very well because she doesn't usually do her marketing here since the supermarket opened in the mall and I was surprised and pleased to see her.'

The grocer smiled to show how pleased he was. 'I also remember that day,' he said, 'because a van driver came up with a delivery and he started talking about having just seen the movie actress driving her car. He's a wise-ass sort of kid and I was worried he wouldn't know who Ann West was and might say something dirty about her sister.'

'And did he?'

'No, but I was worried. You know how these young guys are. He might have blurted out anything about Julia Naundorff's tits or something.'

Ann had apparently spent some time talking to the grocer.

'She was going to make lemonade,' he said. 'Real lemonade. That's why she wanted lemons.'

There was a Polish bakery a few doors down from the grocer's. Ann had gone there that morning.

Evie Placta in the bakery remembered Ann because she wasn't much of a regular customer there either.

'Did she do it?' Evie said. 'Did she kill her sister?'

Parker hadn't announced anything about Julia Naundorff's death, but word had obviously got out. It would have been helped by Evie Placta being Phyllis Skypeck's cousin.

'If she was here buying bread,' Parker said, 'she didn't do it.'

'Rolls too,' Evie said, 'she bought rolls. She spent so much time picking them out you'd think they were something more than rolls.'

Evie seemed to be surprised at customers who took a lot of time making a purchase. At the supermarket at the mall they grabbed things quickly off the shelves, but when they came to Evie's bakery they stood around talking. Evie didn't seem to understand that that was one of the reasons why they came to her, instead of going to the supermarket.

'No,' Evie said, 'her sister was alive then because a kid who drives a delivery van came in to buy some jelly doughnuts. He'd seen the sister in her California car. He started talking about how good-looking she was, no matter that she was old. I watched Ann, to see if she'd be jealous, but she only smiled. But I knew she must be worried about having her big Hollywood sister to stay, because of all the make-up she was wearing just to buy a loaf of bread. I thought maybe she was in competition with the movie star, all made up like that in the morning.'

58

They remembered Ann at the garage where they regularly serviced the old jeep.

The mechanic remembered her very well because only a week before he'd repaired the clutch, but Ann said it was slipping again.

'I tried it out then and there,' the mechanic said, 'but it was working perfectly OK.'

He remembered that was some time around 10 o'clock when Ann came in with the jeep and he'd spent half an hour looking for the trouble. Ann had stood around watching him work. She was interested in car engines.

Whitey Gotton's tackle shop was another place where Ann said she'd been.

'What do you want to know this for, Boomer?' Whitey said.

'Police business.'

'An alibi?' Whitey said. 'She's got an alibi. She was here. She came in sometime after 10.30 and stayed until just after 11, telling me my nieces should come up for a swim. It was nice of her, only it didn't turn out too good. I wish now it hadn't happened. The girls seeing that body in the lake.'

The mother of the three girls was Whitey's sister. Her husband had run off with a waitress from Lobo's bar. Whitey's sister was a nervous wreck. Whitey had tried to help out, taking the three kids off her hands as much as he could.

Whitey's store was cluttered, but he still made room on one wall for photographs from his great days as a pitcher in the Majors.

Parker thought it would be polite to look at the pictures. There were photos of Whitey winding up on the pitcher's mound and of Whitey delivering a pitch. Then there were pictures of Whitey and celebrities. The President of the United States had his picture taken with Whitey. There were photos of Whitey with movie actors. Some of the pictures on the wall were framed pages from newspapers.

Whitey had had a lot of big write-ups. In one newspaper photograph, he was giving an actress an autographed baseball. Parker read the name of the actress in the photo caption. It was Julia Naundorff.

'You knew her?' Parker asked. 'You knew Julia Naundorff?'

'No, I didn't know her,' Whitey said. 'I didn't know her and I didn't know the President of the United States.'

14

Parker and Davy got H. P. Spendlove's room number at the College Inn reception desk and came up unannounced, but Spendlove didn't seem surprised to see them.

'Come in,' he said, just as if he had invited them up.

Spendlove was thin and middle-aged, with large round glasses that looked too big for his narrow face. The glasses had been broken and were repaired with a piece of tape. The tape wasn't too clean. He was wearing a crumpled dark suit that was too big for him, as if he had lost a lot of weight or it had once belonged to a bigger man. He had a black tie that would almost have been a sign of mourning for Julia Naundorff except for the neon red stripe across it.

The room was small and cramped, not one of the College Inn's best. Spendlove's suitcase was in the middle of the floor.

Davy asked, 'Are you leaving?'

'No,' the man said, 'I never unpacked.'

Somehow that seemed to fit with his appearance. Parker remembered the apologetic voice of H. P. Spendlove on the answerphone.

'You're waiting for the funeral?' Davy said. 'You going to go to that?'

'I thought I should,' Spendlove said.

'I'll bet you do,' Davy said. 'You're going to be a rich man now that Julia Naundorff's dead.'

'I'm not going to be rich,' Spendlove said. 'Julia was practically broke, that's why she crept back to her sister's house. Not that it was her sister's. Julia owns the house. I suppose it is worth something, but Ann West gets the house. I'm getting something a lot smaller.'

'How much?' Davy asked.

'I don't know,' Spendlove said, 'but I'll be very surprised if it comes to $30,000.'

'People have been murdered for less,' Davy said.

'I only said $30,000 because it was the first figure that came into my head,' Spendlove said. 'She was a great woman, it would be wonderful if I could see her again.'

'I suppose you could,' Davy said, 'she's in the township morgue.'

'I don't mean there,' Spendlove said and he seemed quite cross. 'I mean here.'

'You do?' Davy said, and he became anxious as though Spendlove might be dangerous.

Parker said, 'Mr Spendlove believes in reincarnation, Davy.'

'That's right,' Spendlove said. 'Julia Naundorff was also a believer. That was the interest we shared. There was nothing else between us, at least not in this life.'

'You met in the past?' Parker asked.

'We thought that we might have,' Spendlove said. 'We had that feeling.'

'Jesus,' Davy said, 'when you were a king in Babylon and she was a Christian slave?'

'You're sceptical,' Spendlove said. 'I don't mind. I'm used to it. But more people believe in reincarnation than do in Christianity.'

'Is that a fact?' said Davy, who didn't believe in anything much outside of a woman coming across when you took her out to eat anything that cost more than ten dollars.

'Oh yes,' Spendlove said. He seemed about to try to sell Davy a tract on the subject.

'Mr Spendlove,' Parker said, 'we have reason to believe that Julia Naundorff was murdered.'

'Not drowned? I thought a man in a boat saw her fall into the water.'

'That's something we've got to go into,' Parker said.

'Yes,' Davy said, 'maybe the man in the boat didn't see what he thought he saw.'

'You went to the farmhouse in Old Compton,' Parker said. 'You were there that morning. What time was that?'

'About 10 o'clock, but I didn't see anything,' Spendlove said. 'I called at the house but no one was home.'

'We've only got your word for that,' Davy said.

'Well,' Spendlove said, 'as a matter of fact you could also have *Ed's Township Cab*'s word for it.'

Parker noticed that Spendlove dropped his hesitant, apologetic manner when he said this, he was so pleased about having a witness. And he ought to be, Parker thought, after all, we're setting him up for a murder.

'You took a cab to Julia Naundorff's?' Davy said.

'I had to,' Spendlove said. 'I don't drive. I was once in a very serious car crash.'

'In another life?' Davy asked.

'No, in Framingham,' Spendlove said, and once again he seemed very superior, despite the crumpled suit and cheap necktie. Spendlove was like a man who had once tried to look sharp on not much money, but had now given up. The sun shining through a window glistened on Spendlove's glasses so Parker couldn't see the man's eyes. He looked sinister, then Parker saw the tape on the frame of the glasses and Spendlove didn't seem so sinister any more, only poor. No doubt about it, $30,000 would be a lot of money to him.

'This room,' Davy said, 'it's kind of cramped, for a man like you.'

It was obvious from the way Davy said *for a man like you* that he was thinking of the money Spendlove would now inherit. Davy obviously didn't believe that a movie star would leave only $30,000.

Spendlove was not put off. 'Yes,' he said, 'I've asked Mr Blanchard, the manager, to find me something bigger, if I'm going to stay for the funeral.'

'So that's why your suitcase is packed?' Davy said.

'I told you, I always have it packed. I was once in a hotel fire.'

'In Framingham?' Davy said.

'No, in another life,' Spendlove said and this time Parker saw the man wasn't being superior, he looked very sad remembering the fire in the hotel in the other life.

'You remember a lot of things from your past lives?' Davy said.

'A few things,' Spendlove said.

'But not Julia Naundorff?'

'No, like I said, we only had a feeling.' Spendlove seemed very sad about not being able to remember Julia Naundorff from a past life.

'That's too bad,' Davy said. 'It would be a whole lot better remembering a good-looking woman like that, than a fire in a hotel in Framingham.'

'The fire wasn't in Framingham,' Spendlove said, 'it was in a hotel in Budapest. In 1894.'

'I suppose you were a hotshot guy back then in Budapest?' Davy asked.

'I was a salesman,' Spendlove said. 'I sold brushes and household cleaners. I wasn't from Budapest. I was from Vienna. That's why I was staying in a hotel.'

'A brush salesman,' Davy said, 'weren't you ever anything interesting?'

Spendlove got a look on his face as though he had been asked that question many times.

'I'm afraid not,' he said. He smiled, but Davy didn't.

'And Julia Naundorff,' Davy said, 'a woman like that, she must have been something fairly big-time in her past lives?'

Spendlove smiled, only a brief upward movement of the lips. The sun reflected on his glasses and he became once again sinister.

'It's the soul that counts,' he said. 'Julia Naundorff had a big-time soul.'

'And a very dead body,' Davy said, 'we've got to concern ourselves with the fact that she was murdered and you are the one person to benefit most from her death.'

'I'm shattered by her death,' Spendlove said. 'No one could feel it more than I.'

His face became incredibly sad. Parker thought that the brush salesman from Vienna must have been very good at commiserating with a customer's grief.

'We're going to check that taxicab story,' Davy said. 'If it doesn't wash, you're going to hear about it.'

'I've nothing to hide,' Spendlove said. 'I tell you, I didn't see Julia Naundorff there. I didn't see her or anyone else, not the thief who was killed, nor the men in the boat.'

There was hysteria in Spendlove's voice. He sat looking as if he might start twitching.

'Is there anything else?' he asked. 'I'm not well today. I'm feeling ill, like I'm coming down with something.'

'No,' Parker said, 'there's nothing else.'

As Parker and Davy went out of the College Inn, Davy said, 'He's nervous. Maybe he's been done for murder in a past life and remembers not liking it very much.'

'He's got a reason for wanting Julia Naundorff dead,' Parker said, 'but how could he do it? How could anyone have done it? The man in the boat didn't see anyone on the boatdock but Julia Naundorff.'

'If he's telling the truth,' Davy said.

15

Jack Coolidge, the man in the boat who saw Julia Naundorff fall, was staying at the Lake House Hotel with Sally Sallas, the man who hadn't seen anything.

Parker and Davy went to see them.

'This is very important,' Parker said to Coolidge. 'If you saw anything at all, you must remember.'

'He told you what he saw,' Sallas said.

'We mean anything extra,' Davy said. 'Sometimes a man sees something and he doesn't know what he's seeing, until later when he thinks it over.'

'I simply happened to glance towards the shore,' Coolidge said. 'I didn't take in anything, except I saw there was a good-looking woman on the boatdock.'

'There you are,' Davy said, 'that's something new that you saw.'

'What do you mean?' Coolidge asked.

'You saw that the woman was good-looking. You didn't mention her looks before.'

'Didn't he?' Sallas said.

'No,' Davy said.

'I thought he did,' Sallas said. 'I think I can remember Jack saying how good-looking the woman was before she fell into the lake.'

'I wish you wouldn't interrupt, Mr Sallas,' Davy said. 'After all, you didn't see anything.'

Parker could tell that Davy was trying to be polite because Sallas was an important man, or at least came from Hollywood where there were many famous men.

'I'm only trying to get it clear,' Sallas said. 'The trouble with you cops is that you always try to make a man feel in the wrong.'

'We don't think Mr Coolidge did anything wrong,' Davy said.

'I mean generally,' Sallas said, 'the way the police behave in a general fashion, assuming guilt.'

Coolidge said, 'I don't actually remember what she looked like. She was a woman in a bathing suit.'

'Sure,' Sallas said, 'a woman in a bathing suit, that's all he saw. At that distance he wouldn't see any particulars. He couldn't even see that it was Julia.'

'Listen,' Davy said to Sallas, 'what are you, his lawyer? Let him do his own talking. He's a Hollywood writer, he's used to words.'

'That's how much you know,' Sallas said, 'the writers, they can hardly get a word out standing on their two legs talking. They can't make a pitch.'

'A pitch?' Davy said. 'We're not after a pitch. It's the truth we want.'

'And besides,' Sallas said, 'Jack's an artist. Let him go on long enough, he'll start telling you the colour of the eyes of the woman he saw two hundred yards away, and the sunlight shining on her face and the breeze playing with her hair.'

Parker smiled. Sallas said, 'You're smiling, but you don't say much. You let this one do all the harassing of an innocent witness who has told you everything already.'

'I'm sorry,' Parker said, 'I'm not a real cop. I'm an invention of the mayor's.'

'A politically appointed chief of police?' Sallas said. He looked at Coolidge as if he were saying that they had landed themselves in a hick town where anything might happen.

Davy said to Coolidge, 'You didn't happen to see a man walking down the lawn from the house to the boatdock? A man in a cheap suit that was hanging on him like it belonged to two other guys?'

'Boy,' Sallas said, 'there's a cop talking. You got a suspect already, have you? And you want Jack's help pinning the rap on him?'

'She was struck on the head,' Parker said. 'The blow killed her. She was dead when she entered the water. What time were you there when she fell in?'

'He don't know,' Sallas said. 'But it seemed to me like I had been out there all my entire life.'

'Were you there at 10 o'clock?' Davy asked Coolidge.

'That's the time the guy in the cheap suit was there, is that right?' Sallas said. 'You want Jack to condemn that cheap-suit guy by saying he saw her go in at 10 o'clock?'

Coolidge said, 'I lost track of the time. We tried a number of places, but the fish weren't biting. We got to that cove early and then we left it and then a while later we came back to try it again. I can't remember when we saw her go in. I'm sorry I can't help you any more, we were just fishing.'

'It's the truth,' Sallas said. 'What else would we be doing out in a boat with a couple of rods and reels?'

'It's something of a coincidence,' Parker said, 'that the two men who happened to know Julia Naundorff were there when she was killed.'

'Now you've graduated,' Sallas said, 'you're not the mayor's invented policeman any more, you're the real thing, accusing a couple of innocent bystanders.'

'You didn't know you were fishing near Julia Naundorff's house?' Parker asked.

'Yeah,' Davy said, 'that's some coincidence.'

'Honest,' Sallas said, 'we didn't have any idea. We knew of course she'd escaped to her stepsister's farm. We knew that. I came up to talk to her. I brought Jack along to convince her, but we hadn't been to the stepsister's place yet. We were saving that for the next day.'

'Escaped?' Parker said. 'Who was Julia Naundorff escaping from?'

'I mean escape in a general sense,' Sallas said. 'Away

from the pressures of movie land. There wasn't anyone after her. At least not that I know of. She did have some dodgy friends. I told her they weren't the kind of people she should associate with, but she never listened.'

'Dodgy friends?' Parker said.

'Mobsters,' Sallas said, 'they like being seen with a movie star, and she thought it was funny knowing them.'

'Jesus,' Davy said and he looked at Parker. Parker understood the look. They were out of their league if the Mob was involved.

'I told her,' Sallas said, 'there wasn't anything funny about it, that those sort of guys were dangerous, they get all sorts of crazy ideas, you never know what they'll do.'

'Was she in trouble with them?' Parker asked.

'I don't know. If so, she never told me. She was edgy, but I thought it was just in a general way and had nothing to do with anything specific, except of course her career had gone to hell.'

'Was she broke?' Davy asked.

'Not what you'd call broke,' Sallas said, 'but she wasn't worth millions any more.'

'Maybe down to her last million, eh?'

Both he and Parker were thinking that H. P. Spendlove might be completely wrong with his $30,000.

Coolidge had been sitting quietly, not saying anything. Now he said, 'There wasn't anyone there. There was a breeze. I saw the branches swaying in the breeze. I can't remember anything that I haven't already told you.'

16

'The Mob,' Davy said, 'they've got strange new ways of killing people. They give a guy a poison cigar. They do all sorts of things, nobody ever knows, except the guy is dead and nobody can point a finger.'

Davy was in the station in North Holford talking to Georgie Stover.

Parker was across the room on the telephone trying to find out about aircraft that might have been flying over the lake at the time Julia Naundorff was killed. He had an idea that maybe something had dropped from a plane and killed her.

There was nothing really to connect Julia Naundorff's odd death with the murders of Billy Zoots and Elroy Green, which had been straightforward sort of killings, one with a knife and the other by strangulation. Parker had simply joined up the three deaths because Billy Zoots and Elroy Green were involved in the robbery at Ann West's house. And they were also connected in his mind because they all had yellow hair, but of course that wasn't enough reason even for an invented policeman. But the boys could have witnessed Julia Naundorff's death and that would be reason enough for the killer to get rid of them.

The death of Julia Naundorff was mysterious and now he had Sal Sallas' talk of Julia Naundorff's Mob connections. Parker couldn't see himself going to Las Vegas to interview men called Lucky and Fingers. Of course, if the Mob was involved they would, presumably, have crossed state lines to get from wherever they were to Old Compton to kill Julia Naundorff and that made it a federal case, the FBI could be called in. That, Parker thought, might be for the best. It would relieve him of responsibility. He had only accepted the job as police chief because he needed the work and it had looked like a soft touch because, after all, nothing very much ever happened in a place like North Holford township, even though it took in a large area around the lake. The city of Holford, where many crimes were committed, was out of Parker's jurisdiction. He thought he'd have a sleepy time policing the township, keeping the cops from stealing things and beating up suspects, but that was not proving to be the case.

It was not easy finding out about flights over the lake. The scheduled airlines tried to be helpful, but they had to check flight paths. There were often diversions because of the weather or a fault arising. Luckily the weather had been clear and calm all along the Eastern seaboard that morning, but a plane on a flight from Manchester, England, to Los Angeles had developed engine trouble and had diverted to Boston. It had flown over the lake. Parker thought he had discovered the cause of Julia Naundorff's death. He imagined a piece of the damaged plane breaking off and falling unnoticed to earth. He saw it rather like parts of his own old DeSoto falling out of the engine.

He had to make several calls to check it.

'Do you mean,' a man on the phone said, 'did some piece of metal, like a nut or a bold or a screw come off the plane? It was at twenty thousand feet, it would have driven a hole through anything it hit.'

'What if it simply grazed a person?'

'Grazed?' the man said. 'Coming down from twenty thousand feet? Besides, there's no record of anything falling off the plane.'

Parker didn't trust such records. When he was a practising lawyer, he had investigated many insurance cases and nothing was ever said to be wrong with an engine or an appliance until he had refused to take no for an answer and looked further.

Across the room Davy and Georgie Stover were still talking about the Mob. Georgie Stover had seen Sal Sallas and he agreed with Davy that Sallas looked and talked like a man who had connections with the Mob, perhaps was even a member of the Mob himself.

'What do you think, Boomer?' Davy asked.

'I haven't really thought about it,' Parker said.

He was thinking about something small falling to earth and striking Julia Naundorff. It would be a very modern sort of death. Or perhaps not, maybe it would be like something out of the Middle Ages, a piece of the sky falling down.

When they pulled Julia Naundorff out of the lake, they had been too busy looking at how beautiful she was to take much notice of anything else. Plus, they had thought it was a case of drowning. They hadn't been looking for airplane parts or pieces of a meteor.

'I'm going back to that boatdock,' Parker said.

'To see Ann West?' Davy said.

'To see something.'

'You want me to come along?' Davy said.

'No.'

'Three's a crowd,' Davy said. 'You've seen Ann West,' he said to Georgie Stover, 'she's a looker. Boomer's interested.'

'I won't be long,' Parker said, 'but if you've got the time, could you try to locate Spa Johnson, see if he's found out anything yet about someone with expensive jewellery to sell.'

Parker left the station. He was feeling almost good. If the death of Julia Naundorff had been an accident, however bizarre, Parker would be on firm ground again with small-time thieves killing one another. Someone, of course, was going to have to pay for the murders of Billy Zoots and Elroy Green. No matter what sort of useless, anti-social characters they were, and unsightly too with their bleached blond hair, they had a right to life, liberty and the pursuit

71

of happiness so long as they weren't caught at it. The good citizens of the township might think the world a better place with Billy Zoots and Elroy Green out of it, but Parker couldn't think that way even if he wanted to, which he didn't.

17

In the fields around the house in Old Compton, Parker saw figures working in the bright sunshine. He stood and watched for a moment, but could catch no sight of Ann West among them.

He didn't go to the house, although he wished very much to see her. He walked down the lawn to the boatdock and started his search, going slowly up and down, doubled over, with his head bent trying to find any alien object that had fallen from the sky. The odds against it being a bit of a meteor were probably ridiculous, and that also seemed to rule out it being a piece of an airplane, at least from a big plane belonging to a major airline. There were other planes, however, that flew over the lake. There were, for example, pontoon planes moored there. The pilots, most of them young, were sometimes irresponsible. They flew tourists in these pontoon planes, giving them an aerial view of the lake. There was no telling what one of these young pilots or their passengers might throw out of a plane. There was no record of their flights. They simply took off, like someone would casually take a boat out. Parker had yet to question any of these pilots. There was a base across the lake where the planes were moored and if he didn't find anything here, he'd have to go to them.

The canvas on the boatdock was relatively new. He could find no odd objects on it, or any hole where something fell from the sky. He was down now on his hands and knees, crawling across the dock. He could see nothing suspicious.

Parker stood up, feeling his back stiffen. Then he saw there was a place where a man could hide and not be seen. It was so obvious that Parker felt stupid only realising it now. The lake itself was a big hiding place. All a killer had to do was keep out of sight under the water until it was time to strike. But to strike with what? The only thing Parker could think of was a slingshot. A kid's weapon. He wondered if in the end they'd find out the Wilson kid had done it.

His attention was drawn to a small black and white dog running across the lawn towards him barking.

'Moll,' Parker said, bending down to greet her.

She jumped at him. She was friendly. Her tail whirled about with the excitement of finding someone new. She had white socks on her paws and a white chest, and there was a white diamond on the back of her head. The contrast with the glossy blackness of the rest of her coat was very pretty.

'Hello, girl,' Parker said, patting her head and stroking her under the chin. His old dog Rags, the Norfolk terrier, had liked that. Parker was not familiar with Staffordshire bull terriers, he had always thought them rather fierce, but this one was extremely playful, with dark, merry eyes and a long red tongue that hung out of her mouth in a playful way.

Parker looked up the lawn, but couldn't see Ann West. Then he heard someone calling the dog. Moll, however, stayed with Parker.

'I don't want you to get in trouble,' he said, but she stayed by him, her tail spinning with pleasure.

Parker looked back to the house. He saw a familiar figure coming down the lawn. It was Spa Johnson.

'What are you doing here?' he asked.

'I came to check on the description of the jewellery,' Spa said. 'Then the pooch got loose.'

He bent down and patted the dog.

'You go out pestering witnesses,' Parker said, 'you should tell me first.'

'I wasn't pestering,' Spa said. 'The description of the jewellery Miss West wrote down, it was confusing.'

'OK,' Parker said.

Ann West appeared on the lawn. Moll turned and ran, with the odd three-legged run of her breed, to her mistress. When she reached her, she turned and ran back to Parker and Spa as they walked up from the dock.

Ann West was once again dressed for the fields, without make-up of any sort. But Parker thought she was a splendid sight, fitting in perfectly with the sunny day and the old farmhouse, which also looked magical in the bright June light. She wore jeans and although her shirt was baggy, he could see her full breasts with the nipples rather prominent. She seemed completely unconscious of this and stood close to him, talking of the dog and now and then leaning down to stroke Moll, then coming upright again and brushing her blonde hair back from her long, grey eyes.

Parker tried not to look directly at her. He knew his voice sounded strange and was giving him away. He forced himself to turn and face her. He could feel his head swimming. He wished Spa wasn't there to see him being foolish. It was really ridiculous suddenly to feel this way at his age, and with his sorry background and dismal prospects for the future. He had no money. He had never had any money. This did not normally bother him, except every now and then when he met a marvellous woman and realised he had no way of capturing and holding her interest.

Ann didn't seem to notice his discomfort. She was telling Spa of a dog show that was coming up and her hopes for Moll doing well. She was, apparently, too playful to stand in a proper way for the judges. Ann turned to Parker and she smiled and Parker could feel himself going red, thinking that she had guessed his secret and was amused by it. Spa, Parker could see, was also amused.

Parker began to tell her, in a halting voice, repeating himself very often and realising how much of a hick cop he must sound, about the theory of something having been dropped from a plane. As he told it, he realised how far-fetched it must seem, and he saw Spa wink at her. They think I'm loonytunes, Parker thought.

But Ann became interested.

'That's incredible,' she said. 'Could it be true?'

Parker was about to tell her he really didn't think it could be, when she interrupted him.

'I hope it is,' she said. 'I can't stand thinking it could be murder. I want it to be an accident.'

'Of course,' Parker said. He dared look at her. Her face was glowing with health from working in the fields and her yellow hair was even more yellow from the sun. It was like honey and not the startling yellow of the three corpses. He tried to remember Julia Naundorff and the two dead men, that was, after all, why he was here; but he found it difficult with Ann standing there, looking so full of life.

Spa said, 'I guess I better get going.'

They watched him walk back up the lawn.

'Who *is* he?' Ann asked. 'He's not like a cop, but I suppose you aren't either.'

'He's helping out. Did he pester you?'

'Only a bit.'

'Women like him,' Parker said.

'Do they?'

'Oh yes, that's his trouble. His brother told me.'

Then he started telling her how he also hoped Julia Naundorff's death had been an accident. Although it was unwise to say it. he spoke of the difficulties of finding her sister's killer – if, in fact, she had been murdered. He told her about interviewing Jack Coolidge and Sal Sallas.

'It *is* a coincidence them being on the water,' he said, 'but I can't see what motive they'd have for killing her.'

'Yes,' Ann said. She seemed no longer interested. She was watching Moll, who was whirling about, attempting to catch her own tail.

'Mr H. P. Spendlove,' Parker said, 'he's a sinister-seeming guy. If he's the murderer, you'd think he'd try not to look so much like one. And he's the one with the motive. He keeps saying your sister won't leave much more than $30,000. But now we learn from her agent, Sal Sallas, that she was worth considerably more than that.'

'I've no idea what she was worth,' Ann West said.

'The money of course,' Parker said, 'creates suspects; or at least a suspect.'

'It must be very difficult,' Ann said, 'with all the possibilities. It makes my head spin thinking about it.'

'I guess I should take first things first,' Parker said.

He was confused. He wished he could stop talking and simply look at her, perhaps sit down on the grass opposite her and gaze at her, maybe holding her hands.

He said, 'Billy Zoots and Elroy Green, I'll have to concentrate on them. I'll have more of a chance with them, especially since a woman named Maria Esperanza, a fortune-teller, saw someone in the backyard at Liberty Street. But whether or not those murders are connected with your sister's death, I don't know.'

He looked at her when he said this and she had turned to watch her dog and wasn't able to see the look on his face. Now she faced him.

'I want to forget it,' she said. 'Is that terrible of me?'

'No, certainly not, only natural.'

He was looking directly at her and she was looking at him and nothing dreadful happened.

But he began chattering away again in a nervous fashion, feeling his mouth go dry, so he had trouble pronouncing some words; he tripped over the name Maria Esperanza when he was telling her again about the fortune-teller having seen someone in the backyard at Liberty Street.

76

'I must come to the station,' Ann said, 'and try to identify the jewellery and see what's still missing.'

'Yes,' Parker said and he reddened because his *yes* had been too enthusiastic, as if she had agreed to go out to dinner with him and not merely said she'd help with the investigation. He had to look away and then when he looked again he thought he saw a smile disappearing from her face.

She knows the way I feel about her all right, Parker said to himself.

18

Spa was in the station when Parker returned.

'He hasn't found a thing,' Davy said to Parker. 'I said he'd be wasting everyone's time.'

'I've been everywhere,' Spa said, 'I seen everyone. They don't know a thing.'

'Or they're not saying,' Davy said.

'That could be the case,' Spa said, 'but I don't believe so. Those boys like to brag about what they know. They can't help it. That's what made Elroy stand out – he could keep his mouth tight.'

'He told someone,' Davy said. 'They knew he had stolen stuff.'

'Elroy,' Spa said, 'he always had stolen stuff, he had nothing but stolen stuff, he never bought a thing.'

'Keep looking,' Parker said.

'I will,' Spa said, 'but what's this job at the Lakeside Players?'

Parker had forgotten about that.

'I'm sorry,' he said, 'I haven't seen Dick Doyle yet. I'll drop round and see him today.'

'Get out of here,' Davy said to Spa. 'Go on, get out before I think of something to charge you with.' Then he turned to Parker and said, 'Maria Esperanza called, she's coming in.'

'She doesn't have to. I'd go to Liberty Street and save her the trip.'

'She wants to come. She says she can't stand staying in the place now. She says it's got bad vibrations since the murder. She's nervous. She's thinking of moving out.'

But when Maria Esperanza, wearing a tight maroon skirt and a form-hugging white blouse, arrived, Parker found that Davy had got the story wrong. She wanted to move into Elroy Green's room at Estelle Ritter's house as soon as the police were finished with it.

'It's the vibrations,' she said, 'they're very strong.'

'Don't you get frightened?' Georgie Stover asked. He was looking at her, in her white blouse and tight maroon skirt, as though he'd never seen anything like her before, and probably he hadn't.

'Elroy Green's death was terrible and his spirit is disturbed, but there's nothing to fear from a departed spirit.'

'I'd be frightened,' Georgie said.

Maria Esperanza was a good-looking woman, but her bleached blonde hair did not suit her dark, Latin complexion. Parker was reminded of Billy Zoots, Julia Naundorff and Elroy Green. That startling yellow hair was proving unlucky in North Holford.

He asked her about herself. She was half Puerto Rican, half Irish, born in Massachusetts. Esperanza was her mother's name. She said her father was an Irish-American called Murphy, at least she thought it was Murphy, she had never seen him.

'From the time I was a child,' she said, 'I had this feeling for other things.'

Parker could see Davy standing on the other side of the

room watching her. He hoped Davy wouldn't laugh. But Davy was more interested in how she was put together than what she was saying.

'I dropped out of high school,' she said, 'I worked on the checkout at the Stop and Shop, but I had trouble with a boy. It was strange, I always knew he'd be trouble. He had a dark aura. That's a thing round his head. Even back then I could sometimes see it on a person.'

Her eyes went to the top of Parker's head. If she saw an aura, her eyes didn't give her away.

'I went to Boston,' she said. 'I was dancing at a place in the Combat Zone. Acrobatic sort of dancing, not stripping – but we didn't have much on, and nothing on the top. We were topless, that's what the law allowed.'

Parker could see Davy's eyes light up.

She said, 'The customers come and shove dollar bills, sometimes five or ten dollar bills, in your G-string. It wasn't bad when you're a kid and everything seems like a joke. You sit down sometimes, have a drink with them between numbers. But all the time I was getting emanations. "If I had your brain, I'd go back to school," a friend told me. So I did. I thought, "Hell, I can get a job working in an office." But the emanations continued, getting stronger.'

Parker felt like a doctor hearing a patient's symptoms. He felt he had to listen to her story to see how much of a reliable witness she would make. She was so matter of fact about her emanations that she no longer seemed comic. Parker was reminded of something. Maria Esperanza was like H. P. Spendlove, speaking of his past life as a brush salesman in Vienna.

'I started reading about it,' she said. 'I wasn't too keen about setting up as a fortune-teller. I mean, they always seemed like fat, crazy old phoneys. But the emanations got so strong. I mean just walking down a street and seeing someone, I could tell things. I went to a doctor – to a couple of doctors. They couldn't help me. Then I met a man who was a help. He wasn't concerned with my field, but he said he understood. He was the one who suggested I take it up full-time. That was a long time ago. He was a famous man in his field of study. He writes books about reincarnation. Maybe you've heard of him – H. P. Spendlove.'

She must have seen the look on Parker's face.

'Yes,' she said, 'the same one. He's been in the news lately. He's the one who's inherited all that money from the actress who died.'

'When did you come to North Holford?' Parker asked.

'In the spring.' She glanced around the room, recrossing her legs. The skirt she wore was so tight, it bulged at the thighs. 'Say,' she said, 'can I smoke in here? I'm all nerves, I need a cigarette.'

'Sure,' Parker said, 'go ahead.'

She went through her handbag looking for her cigarettes.

'Why did you come to North Holford?' Parker asked.

She held a cigarette to her mouth. It seemed incredibly sexy seeing the smoke curl out from her lips. She wore maroon lipstick to match her skirt. The end of the cigarette was stained with it. 'I came for my health. For the clean air. I was getting ill in Boston. I had a nice place there, but I was getting ill.'

The door of the station opened and Ann West walked in.

'Sorry, have I come at a bad time?' she said seeing Maria Esperanza there.

'No,' Parker said, 'it's all right.'

But it really wasn't proper to have someone there listening to a witness. There was little he could do about it. The station was so small. There wasn't a room where Parker could take anyone to talk in private.

'Show Miss West the jewellery from Liberty Street,' Parker said to Davy.

As Parker listened to Maria Esperanza tell her life story, he was aware of Ann across the room and he kept glancing over to her. The clairvoyant smiled with a curl of white smoke coming from her maroon lips. She was amused rather than annoyed by him being distracted by the good-looking woman. They were a complete contrast, Ann West and Maria Esperanza. Ann was a creature of the outdoors, while Parker could not imagine Maria Esperanza anywhere but in darkened rooms or on a stage, with men's faces looking up at her out of the dark while she did amazing acrobatic things.

She said she liked reading tarot cards.

'I could do a reading for you sometime,' she said to Parker.

He saw Ann hear this and smile. She had also smiled when she caught him looking at her while they spoke on the lawn at Old Compton. He was proving to be a source of amusement for her.

'That would be nice,' he said, 'but I want to know what you saw in the backyard when Elroy Green was killed.'

This, after all, was why she was here. The story of her life was not the point, except where it might affect her ability to convince a jury.

'I'm still not sure what I saw,' she said. 'Often a person will see something and not take it in, because they're busy doing or thinking about something else. They don't realise what they've seen until later.'

Parker had heard this before. It was what Davy had said to Jack Coolidge and Sally Sallas.

'Do you know what you've seen now?' Parker asked.

Maria Esperanza shook her head. 'No, I don't know.' She looked about for somewhere to put her cigarette. Georgie Stover gave her an ashtray. He had been standing watching her. Parker wondered if Georgie ever went down to Boston's Combat Zone to see girls. Georgie was too young ever to have seen Maria Esperanza. Maybe, Parker thought, Georgie's simply interested in the supernatural. There was something spooky about Maria Esperanza, and the combination of that and her big body and the sexy look on her face would fascinate a boy like Georgie; it fascinated Parker.

Maria Esperanza stood up. She was tall. Her figure was even more stunning when she was on her feet. Parker could see Georgie and Davy taking her in.

'If it comes to me,' she said, 'I'll let you know.'

'It is rather urgent,' Parker said.

They all watched her as she walked to the door, even Ann West watched.

19

After Maria Esperanza left, Parker showed Ann the jewellery that they'd found in Elroy Green's room.

'At least you've got this back,' Davy said.

'Yes,' Ann said, but she wasn't enthusiastic.

'It looks real good expensive jewellery,' Davy said.

'Everything Julia had was expensive,' Ann said.

'Did your sister have enemies?' Parker asked.

'Not that I know of, but she didn't have any friends. I don't think anyone really liked Julia. She was always playing the Southern belle, which was annoying.' She smiled. 'Do you want me for anything else?' she asked.

'No,' Parker said. He could feel himself reddening again. He looked away from the blonde hair.

'I'll go then,' she said.

The yellow hair swung loose and covered half her face as she rose.

Parker went with her to the door and held it open. He noticed that neither Davy nor Georgie Stover watched her walking across the room the way they had watched Maria Esperanza.

Parker went out to the street with her.

'Is something wrong?' she asked.

He knew he must have been frowning, displaying something, anyway.

'No, nothing at all,' he said. 'I was thinking of something.'

Coolidge, he thought, he might be in it with her. He could be lying when he said he saw Julia fall into the lake. Jack Coolidge was a good-looking guy. He could have got involved in an elaborate plot with Ann West. With Sal Sallas, too. He would also have had to be in on it. Coolidge could be Ann's lover. But what was the motive?

The door to the station was still open. Parker shouted through it, 'I'm going to the Lakeside Players.'

He walked with Ann to her car. A strand of blonde hair fell down across her face. She pushed it away, smiling at Parker. She was standing by the car. It was not the old, dust-covered jeep. It was the new BMW with the California plates, the car Julia Naundorff had gone for a ride in the morning of her murder.

'Did your sister drive this all the way from Los Angeles?'

He had trouble imagining a Hollywood actress putting herself through a trip like that.

'Yes,' Ann said. 'She claimed it gave her time to think.'

This was something new to worry Parker. There was an element of fleeing about a drive like that, three thousand miles across the country. He thought of Julia Naundorff's friends in the Mob. It was better to think of that, than of Ann with Coolidge.

Ann got into the car. She smiled at him again. It was a nervous smile that said how worried she was by the mystery of her stepsister's death and how she understood that Parker was having a difficult time attempting to solve it.

20

Parker drove to the Lakeside Players. The theatre was near the amusement park, but far enough away for the noise of the people screaming as they rode the rollercoaster or the other exciting rides not to disturb the plays too much. Sometimes, however, in the evening, when the doors were open for an interval, the smokers standing outside in the dark could hear the old-fashioned steam organ music from the merry-go-round and it gave them a memory, especially if the play they were attending was complicated, of the simpler pleasures of childhood.

Parker walked through the amusement park to the theatre. He had sad memories of being there with his daughters when they were young and their mother had first left them. There was something tragic about them then, amongst the forced professional jollity of the fairground. He would glance down at their faces and be amazed by their looks of utter boredom as if the speed and sudden twisting motions had no effect. Parker suspected that they had been numbed by their mother leaving them; he had been, there was no reason why they should be any different. On those rare occasions when his wife came to visit the children, her vitality had made her seem a stranger from a foreign country. It was as if she were the young one and Parker and the daughters were immeasurably old.

In the amusement park now children were looking at him because he was so tall. Some pointed at him. He felt like a side-show freak. He thought he must look a sinister figure, like H. P. Spendlove.

Across the way, by a booth in the arcade, he saw Whitey Gotton and his three nieces. He wondered what damage the sight of the dead woman in the water had done to them. Already the nieces would have seen much violence and many dead on television. The violence on TV was good instruction for life, much more practical than Mickey Mouse. But the horror on their faces had been real as they looked down at the dead woman in the water.

Whitey moved with a rolling walk, favouring his burnt-out pitcher's shoulder like another man might favour a crippled leg. Whitey had known Julia Naundorff in Los Angeles. Another elaborate plot, like the one between Ann West and Jack Coolidge, began to form in Parker's head. In this one, Ann West and Whitey Gotton had killed Julia Naundorff. But that didn't explain Coolidge seeing Julia falling into the lake. And once again, what could the motive be?

Parker went past the merry-go-round and down through some pine trees that separated the amusement park from the theatre. The parking lot of the theatre was empty, there was no performance this afternoon, but there was a rehearsal going on.

Dick Doyle saw Parker and motioned to him to go backstage. There was a room there where the actors had drinks after a performance. Doyle, a good-looking Irishman from Dublin, was the general manager of the theatre. The money for the theatre had been put up by a woman from New York called Lillian Hauser. She was said to be Doyle's girl, at least one of his girls, he had a lot of women. They all tried to cure him of drinking. The drink, Parker thought, was part of his Irish charm.

Lillian Hauser was in the room, sitting in a chair reading a play, when Parker and Doyle came in.

Doyle was almost as tall as Parker. They stood talking. Lillian said, 'Will you please sit down. You don't realise how difficult it is sitting here trying to look at you two freaks being so tall.'

Doyle smiled and sat down. He had the handsome looks of an old-fashioned leading man. Lillian was not good-looking, but she was saved from being plain by an intelligent intensity that made people think she might at any moment say or do something interesting. Besides, she had money, and people said she was the driving force behind the theatre, selecting the plays and telling Doyle how he should direct them, not when a rehearsal was in progress but later on, when she and Doyle were alone. Why else, people said, would she sit in the back of the theatre during rehearsals scribbling notes?

Doyle said, 'Somebody told me, Boomer, that you've been looking for things that fell from the sky. Would that be a piece off a flying saucer?'

'We haven't got much time,' Lillian said to Doyle. She was ignoring Parker now that he was seated.

'There's been murders, honey,' Doyle said to her, 'it's real life, it's interesting, it's where the theatre is supposed to come from.'

Lillian made a face. She went back to reading.

'I came here to ask you a favour,' Parker said.

'That's a surprise,' Lillian said without looking up.

'Do you need some summer help?' Parker asked.

'What's this?' Lillian said to Doyle. 'Does he have a girlfriend who wants to go on the stage? Tell him no, we can't start this sort of thing.' She spoke to Doyle as if Parker weren't there.

'Not on stage,' Parker said, 'backstage.'

He spoke to Doyle. He was careful not to look at Lillian. 'It's a young fellow I'm trying to help out.'

He told Doyle about Spa, leaving out how he had come to meet him.

'We can always use someone,' Doyle said.

'Can we?' Lillian said.

'Sure,' Doyle said, 'you know we're short-handed.'

'You mean the ones we've got won't work,' Lillian said. 'Go ahead, hire him, let him burn the damned theatre to the ground.'

Doyle smiled and patted her on the knee. She moved her legs away.

'What about these murders,' she said to Parker, 'is it true Julia Naundorff was also murdered?'

News travels fast in North Holford, Parker thought.

'I knew her,' Doyle said.

'Sure you did,' Lillian said in a sarcastic voice.

'I was in a play with her. In New Haven.'

'In the year dot,' Lillian said.

'We never got to New York.'

'That's a surprise,' Lillian said. Parker could see she was enjoying herself. She put the play she'd been reading down and sat watching them.

Parker went to the front of the theatre with Doyle. The actors who had been rehearsing were sitting about. One of them, a good-looking girl, looked up as Doyle passed by. Doyle tried not to look at her.

Doyle said, 'I have to watch it about Julia with Lillian. In fact I have to watch it about everyone with her. But Julia and I had a thing. We lived together for some time, but I can never mention that to Lillian.'

'You lived with her?'

'Julia and me? Oh yes.'

Doyle smiled a big Irish smile, apparently completely unaware that he had just made himself a suspect.

Well, Parker thought, if he is the murderer, he would act like this.

'Where were you that morning?' Parker said.

'What morning?'

'When Julia Naundorff was killed.'

'Oh yes, of course, I'd be a suspect now, I see,' Doyle sounded very Irish. 'Christ, I don't know,' he said. 'That's the truth. I'll have to think. It'll have to be something that Lillian won't find out about.'

'It'll have to be the truth.'

'Not if Lillian is going to hear about it.'

'You were with a woman?'

'Of course I was with a woman.'

'Try to remember the name of the woman you were with,' Parker said.

As he left, Parker saw Lillian Hauser coming out from back stage. The actors got to their feet. They looked very nervous.

'Dick,' Lillian shouted, 'Dick, where the hell are you? They're ready for that scene at the end of the first act.'

21

So there was someone else in North Holford who knew Julia Naundorff. This new complication worried Parker, although he couldn't see the easy-going Dick Doyle committing murder. But somebody had, and in Julia Naundorff's case he had been so clever that nobody knew how he did it.

H. P. Spendlove was the man with the motive. Parker had been unable to check Spendlove's taxicab alibi because the cab driver who had taken Spendlove to the house in Old Compton was in Holford City Hospital.

Parker told himself that he was being considerate not disturbing the driver, a man called Laporte, but now he felt he couldn't put it off any longer.

He left the station and drove to Holford, which was only six miles away, but was a complete contrast – a dirty mill-town that no longer had any working mills.

When he came into Holford City Hospital the first person he saw was Dr Phyllis Skypeck.

'Christ,' she said, 'I hate being the medical examiner. I hope Stanley gets well soon.'

Stanley Howse, the regular medical examiner, was in a home taking a cure. He drank.

Parker left Phyllis and went to find the taxi driver.

Bart Laporte was a surprise. He was a bearded giant whose muscles bulged inside the flimsy hospital nightshirt. He looked like a professional wrestler. Cab driving, it seemed to Parker, was a ludicrously sedentary occupation for a man like this. If the Holford mills were open, he would be happily employed throwing machinery about. He was in hospital with a suspected bad heart.

Parker told Laporte what he had come for.

'The day Julia Naundorff died and Billy Zoots had his throat cut, do you remember a fare about 10 o'clock in the morning from the College Inn to Ann West's farmhouse in Old Compton?'

'Sure I remember him,' Laporte said.

'How can you be so sure?'

'He was wearing a bow tie.'

There were many things about H. P. Spendlove that Parker thought might make him memorable, but he hadn't thought it would be a bow tie.

'I thought wearing a bow tie he must be an Englishman or something,' Laporte said. 'Is he an Englisher?'

'I don't know. I don't think so.'

'What's wrong? Is he dead too? I read about those deaths, of course, but I haven't taken much notice. Not the way I am.'

'When you took him to the house at Old Compton, what did he do?'

'The guy in the bow tie? He didn't do nothing. There wasn't anybody at home. He was angry, in an English kind of way, on account of he had an appointment.'

'Where?'

'Where what?'

'Where did he have an appointment?'

'At the house in Old Compton. With the actress. He had a date to meet the actress. What's her name? I forget.'

'Julia Naundorff.'

'Oh yeah. Can you imagine me forgetting that? I can't think too good.'

His voice was very small. He fingered the edge of the blanket.

'How'd he know no one was in?' Parker asked.

'They didn't come to the door. Then he walked around.'

'Where to?'

'To the back door, I suppose. And then down to the lake.'

'Did you see him walking down to the lake?'

'Some of the time. I got out of the cab.'

'You didn't see anyone else?'

'I told you, there was no one at home. They didn't answer the door.'

'I mean when Mr Spendlove walked down to the lake. Was there anyone else there?'

'Not that I saw. I wasn't really watching. Besides, he went out of sight.'

'Out of sight?'

'Down a dip in the lawn where I could only see his head and then not even that. What's wrong? Do you think he did it? Jesus, that'd be something. And me up there only feet away.'

22

At the College Inn, Parker asked the girl at the reception desk to ring Spendlove's room. The girl gave Parker one of those superior little smiles that hotel receptionists use and said, 'Mr Spendlove is not in his room right now. He is probably in the lounge. I haven't seen him go out.'

Parker could tell H. P. Spendlove had become a valued customer now that word had got out about him inheriting Julia Naundorff's money. Parker went to the lounge and he could see right away why the cab driver might think

H. P. Spendlove an Englishman. There was something foreign about him anyway. Parker wondered if it was a hangover from the time he was a brush salesman in Budapest. He wasn't wearing a bow tie. The tie he wore today was all black – the cheap red stripe had disappeared – and it was silk and looked expensive. The dark suit he wore also looked rich and then Parker saw it was the same suit he had worn before, but it had been dry-cleaned. Spendlove's shoes had also been given a shine and his shirt was clean, with french cuffs that were held together by expensive gold cufflinks that Parker could not remember from before. The only flaw in Spendlove's presentation was that the suit was still too big for him and the piece of tape that held his glasses together was still dirty.

Parker wondered why a man who had suddenly become so aware of his appearance hadn't got his glasses repaired.

Spendlove was sitting with his slim legs crossed, holding a cup of tea to his lips as if it was something that had been especially sent down to him from somewhere far away.

'Have some tea, Inspector,' he said and his mouth curled at one edge to show that he was being satiric, using the English crime-story rank.

'They tried to fob me off with some inch-thick crockery that looked like something from the Stone Age, but I protested and they found this china hidden in the recesses of the kitchen. I don't suppose the Rotarians or other local dignitaries could tell the difference. But it is Lapsang Suchong and it does deserve something better than a chamberpot.'

Spendlove had been camp before, but not this camp. Parker reckoned it hadn't hit Spendlove then just how rich he was going to be with Julia Naundorff dead. It had hit him now, but his suit still didn't fit.

'Where are you from, Mr Spendlove?' Parker asked.

'Do you mean where was I born?'

The lip curled again at the edge and the glasses glinted in a shaft of sunlight coming through an open window.

'Ohio,' Spendlove said. 'Coffintown, Ohio. That's in the Western Reserve.'

The Western Reserve meant nothing to Parker, but the way Spendlove said it made it seem important.

'Since then,' Spendlove said, 'I've travelled all over the world and lived in many places.'

'Lately you've lived in Boston?'

'That's right. I've got rooms in Commonwealth Avenue.' The way he said *rooms* made it sound old-world and classy. 'Just down from the corner of Exeter Street. By the Harvard Club. Do you know it?'

The way he threw in the Harvard Club made it sound like Spendlove had picked his rooms because it would be convenient when he thought of dropping in.

'No,' Parker said, 'I've never been in it. Are you a Harvard man?'

Spendlove looked at him over his teacup. The sun was no longer glinting off his glasses. Parker could see the small dark-brown eyes observing him closely for a moment. Spendlove moved his head and the sun was reflecting off his glasses again.

'No,' he said, 'I've no association with that seat of learning.'

Parker had a feeling Spendlove might just as easily have said something else.

'I was educated abroad,' he said. 'Mainly educated abroad.'

'Did you know a Miss Maria Esperanza in Boston?'

'No, I don't think I did.' Spendlove put down his teacup. 'Would you like a real drink, Inspector? About this time of day I usually take strong waters. Or are you on duty?'

'I'm on duty, but I'll have a drink.'

'Good for you,' Spendlove said, and for a moment Parker thought he was going to be patted on the knee.

'Miss Maria Esperanza šays she knows you.'

'More people know Tom Fool than Tom Fool knows.'

'She claims she met you a few years ago and that you gave her career advice.'

'Does she? Did I?' He turned, snapping his fingers, signalling to a waitress. It was the same girl who had been working behind the reception desk. She didn't at all seem to mind having fingers snapped at her, at least not by such a classy guy as Spendlove.

'Yes, Mr Spendlove?' she said.

'Drink,' he said, 'strong drink.'

The girl smiled. Spendlove was a character, an eccentric.

'A dry martini, I think,' Spendlove said. 'It is the supreme achievement of American culture. And you?' he added to Parker.

'A beer,' Parker said.

'Of course,' Spendlove said and his glasses managed to glint again. 'About this career advice I was supposed to have given. I give lectures. I'm asked to give talks. Afterwards there are often people, almost always women, who come up to me and ask my advice. I suspect your Maria Esperanza was one of those. Why do you inquire about her, is she a suspect? I thought I was the only one.'

'You're merely the chief suspect,' Parker said.

'Stardom,' Spendlove said, 'fame at last.'

'Are you interested in the theatre?'

'Not until I met Julia. Then, of course, I became keen not so much on the theatre as on the movies. What advice did I give Maria Esperanza?'

'You said she should become a clairvoyant.'

'And did she?'

'Yes.'

'Where? In Boston?'

'Here in North Holford.'

'Oh dear. But I suppose it sounded like a good idea at the time. One really should be careful of the advice one gives the young, they might make a mistake and follow it. A clairvoyant?' He shook his head as though appalled by the idea.

'The Millennium has come, but the altars are broken and the temples lie in ruin and people are ready to believe in anything. But a clairvoyant who hopes to make a living in rural New England is being a bit overly optimistic. Is she helping you with your inquiries? Is she going to read the tarot cards and tell you whodunit?'

'Did you have a close relationship with Julia Naundorff?'

'I don't know what you mean by *close*.'

'You get her money. That seems about as close as it gets.'

'We were never intimate. She telephoned me a lot. At all times of the day or night. She liked to talk late at night.'

'About reincarnation?'

'About anything that happened to cross her mind. She was the physical type and when they get an idea in their heads, it rather overwhelms them. They don't know what to do with it. She was from the South, a simple soul. She tried to pretend that she was a high class Southern belle, but she was from some dirt-poor God's little acre down somewhere on Tobacco Road in deepest Dixie.'

Spendlove smiled to show how good-humoured his snobbery was.

'She called you on the morning she died?' Parker said.

'She left a message for me. I didn't speak to her.'

'She made a date to meet you at the house in Old Compton and then when you got there she'd gone out. Didn't you think that was funny?'

'Funny?'

'Strange.'

'I suppose so.'

Parker said, 'I would think it odd of her to make an appointment, to go to the trouble to leave you a message to come to the house and then for her to go for a drive through North Holford when she knew you'd be going to the house in Old Compton.'

'Driving round North Holford, is that where she was when I went to the house?'

'Yes. If the cab company's time sheets are correct. You went to the house at 10 o'clock. She was driving round North Holford then.'

'And then she came home and went swimming and was drowned?'

'She didn't drown,' Parker said.

'But a man saw her fall into the water,' Spendlove said. 'He didn't see anyone push her and he didn't see a living soul about who could have struck her, but you say she didn't drown. Was it a heart attack? Are you sure your medical examiner knows what he's doing?'

'The medical examiner is a she.'

'Is she experienced?'

'She's only temporary. She's standing in. The other one is ill.'

'Oh,' Spendlove said, and the way he said it and the look on his face when he did made it clear that he thought the hick authorities in North Holford had got it wrong.

'It was murder,' Parker said.

'And what about the dead burglar in the bushes? Was I in time to murder him?' Spendlove asked.

'It's difficult telling an exact time of death,' Parker said. 'You may have been there about that time.'

'Of course I have a motive for getting rid of Julia, but I can't see why I should do in the wretched boy. Unless I was so cross about Julia not being there for me to kill, that I just had to kill someone.'

Parker left Spendlove who was having another dry martini.

Back at the station, Parker put a call through to the police in Coffintown, Ohio. He had to wait some time, but finally he had his answer. There was no H. P. Spendlove on record in Coffintown, Ohio. No H. P. Spendlove had been born there; in fact, no Spendlove at all had ever lived in Coffintown, Ohio.

'By the way,' Parker said, 'what's the Western Reserve?' He could tell the cop in Ohio thought it an odd question.

'It's an old name,' the cop said, 'in the old colonial days Connecticut reserved some land here for its people to move to.'

It was an odd sort of thing for Spendlove to brag about, Parker thought. And there seemed no advantage in saying he was born in Coffintown, Ohio, if he wasn't, unless he was making a joke. If he was, it seemed pretty obscure to Parker. Maybe, Parker thought, Spendlove had been born there in another life.

23

A woman came into the station. She was a tall, big-boned woman with bleached blonde hair the same shade of yellow that the corpses were favouring that summer.

'I want to see Jewel,' she said in a Southern accent. 'I'm a mother,' the big woman said, 'and I've got rights.'

'Why don't you sit down and calm yourself,' Davy said.

'Sit down and calm myself?' the woman said. 'All my life I've sat down and calmed myself and still awful events occurred. Can you imagine how I feel? How I, a *mother*, feels? No of course you can't.'

Parker could smell the perfume the big woman was wearing, and along with the perfume he could smell drink. He had an idea that she was fairly drunk, at least the smell of drink seemed to be beating the perfume. Colour also came into it. She wore several colours that were fighting each other heroically. All this conflict of colours and scents was not very edifying, especially for a woman who kept telling them that she was a mother.

'The mother of who?' Parker said.

'Say,' the woman said, 'are you all right in the head?'

'I don't know,' Parker said, 'at least not for sure.'

'Well you can't be so much of a feeb you can't understand that I want to see Jewel.'

'What's going on?' Parker asked Davy, but Davy only shrugged.

'I'm Kimberly Naundorff,' the big woman said, 'and I want to see Jewel.'

Parker was confused. Then he supposed that the woman was a sister of Julia Naundorff that he hadn't been told about.

'You're related to Julia Naundorff?' he said.

'You bet I am,' the woman said, 'I'm her mother, she's my Baby Jewel.'

Parker thought there must be some mistake. Kimberly Naundorff didn't look old enough to be Julia's mother.

'Say,' the woman said to Davy, 'who is this guy who doesn't know the news?'

'He's the chief of police,' Davy said.

'Where you been,' Kimberly Naundorff said to Parker, 'locked away somewhere? I had my little girl when I was only a child myself, age of fifteen. But Jewel was a love child, that's why she was so lovely, until she turned against me. That's a human tragedy.'

Davy smiled. The woman turned on him.

'It's not funny,' she said, 'she wasn't my little Baby Jewel any more. She became *Julia*, very ritzy, and she refused to see me, but I want to see her now and try to remember her as Baby Jewel. Oh, she was such a charmer then, always singing and dancing, a regular performing child.'

Parker tried not to smile, but it was difficult, the big woman's performance was funny.

He thought that she should legally be Mrs West, but he reckoned there was more prestige in having the same last name as the famous daughter.

97

'Something's going on here,' Kimberly Naundorff said. She sat down, but she still wanted action. 'What's going on? How come my baby's death is suspicious?'

'We're still investigating,' Parker said. 'There're some things we've got to clear up.'

Kimberly Naundorff became even more agitated. Parker was worried that she was going to get up and start storming about the station again. At the same time he was trying to imagine Kimberly Naundorff as Ann West's step-mother. It was a difficult thing to do. It also made him wonder about Mr West, the farmer in Pennsylvania who had brought this woman home one day to be his new wife. Of course she must have been good-looking. She still was, if a trifle overblown for motherhood. It was the yellow hair and the perfume and the drink, also the clothes that didn't spell mother.

'I'm sorry about your daughter,' Parker said.

'What?' the woman said, looking up as though surprised. 'She was never no real daughter to me,' she said. 'Can you imagine getting the Mob, the M. O. B. Mob, to warn me off? What kind of thing is that for a daughter to do to a mother?'

She looked at Parker to see if he was taking in the nastiness of that situation. He could tell she still thought he might be seriously dim-witted.

'Maybe,' she said, 'Miss *Julia* Naundorff outsmarted herself there. Maybe she done something her pals in the Mafia didn't like and they took care of her real good. It could be. It could happen. The M.O.B., they don't monkey around.'

Davy glanced at Parker. Parker knew Davy was keen on the idea of the Mob coming to North Holford. It was the sort of exciting thing that would give him something to talk about for the rest of his life. It would make a difference to his conversation, which was usually restricted to the restaurant he had gone to the night before and how sexy the waitress had been.

'I don't know,' Kimberly Naundorff said. 'When I heard she was coming to live here with that other one, I had an idea something suspicious was happening. Of course her career was all washed up. She hadn't made a picture in a couple of years. She was getting to be a has-been. I guess that's something better than a never-was, but still . . . '

Parker watched as the woman paused, obviously deep in philosophical speculation about life.

'I guess she had her memories,' Kimberly Naundorff said. 'Me, I only had dreams.'

She sat quietly with this thought. Then she became agitated again. 'The first time she done it to me,' she said, 'the first time she rejected me, I hadn't seen her in years. And no phone calls, not even a card. I went to Los Angeles. She'd just made her first big picture then. She didn't want to know me. "Baby Jewel," I said, "it's your Mommie." "Baby Jewel is dead," she said to me. "I'm Julia now. Not Jewel, but Julia." Well Julia is dead now too and I'm still here. That time I first went to Los Angeles to see her, I was working as a waitress in Jackson, Mississippi, and it cost me money to get out West to see her. But did she care?'

She looked at Parker as though expecting him to say something.

'I suppose children can be ungrateful,' Parker said.

'You bet,' she said. 'And you can probably guess how that made me feel.'

'I guess I can,' Parker said.

'No you can't,' she said. 'Nobody who's never been a mother can know what I felt, rejected by my own daughter.'

The big blonde woman was so full of life that Parker had the idea that she might break out in song. There was something unreal about her and her tragedy.

'I guess we can make arrangements for you to see her,' Parker said.

'I wonder,' the woman said, 'I wonder if it'll be worth it. A daughter like that who turned against her own mother.

Still, I got other memories of her when she was my Baby Jewel and we were like that.' She held up two crossed fingers to show how close they had been.

Parker was thinking it must have been a rather tragic time for Ann West when her father brought this woman home to stay. Baby Jewel, the performing child, also must have been an upsetting addition. He was attempting to see the wonderfully blonde and healthy Ann as an unhappy child, when the door of the station opened and Ann came in.

'You took your time,' Kimberly Naundorff said to her. 'I phoned you an hour ago.'

'Well,' Ann said, 'I'm here now, Kim.'

'These cops,' Kimberly Naundorff said, 'won't let me see Baby Jewel.'

Ann looked at Parker.

'I don't think it would be advisable,' Parker said. 'The medical examiner has been looking at her.'

'Looking at her?' Kimberly Naundorff said. 'What do you mean?' Then she paused. 'Oh Jesus,' she said, 'you've been cutting her up, that's awful, that's disgusting for a woman who was a great beauty all her life.'

'It can't be helped,' Ann said.

'You were always jealous of her,' Kimberly Naundorff said. 'I suppose you're happy now, with her dead?'

'Of course I'm not,' Ann said and she placed a hand on the woman's shoulder.

'Julia dead,' Kimberly said. The way she said the name Julia was different now. It was the first time, Parker thought, that she seemed to be referring to a real person. All those comments about Baby Jewel had sounded as though she were talking about a make-believe and slightly comic character, but now Kimberly Naundorff's voice was full of the tragedy of her daughter's death. Parker told himself that the rest of it had been done to mask the pain. She had played the Baby Jewel scene for them because she refused to let strangers see her true feelings. Parker thought that commendable.

'You better come home with me,' Ann said.

'I was going to ask if I could stay with you until the funeral,' Kimberly said, 'but seeing you again, I'm not too sure.'

'Of course you should stay with me,' Ann said, but she didn't sound too pleased about it.

'What?' Kimberly said. 'Do you think sorrow is going to bring us together?' She stood up. She wasn't as tall as Ann, but she was big and dramatic. 'We never got on,' she said. 'We shouldn't kid ourselves just because something bad has happened.'

She turned to Davy. 'Say,' she said, 'you got any kind of a hotel in this place? You got anything that might pass for classy?'

'The College Inn,' Davy said.

'OK,' she said, 'that's for me. You'll find me there. I don't need to go asking charity from relatives.'

Davy went out the door with her. Parker could see them standing in the street with Davy pointing towards the College Inn. She went off, a flash of colours walking down the street on tottering high heels. She's back to playing farce again, Parker thought.

'Well,' Ann said, 'I was willing to help, but you see how she is.'

Parker walked her to the door and then to her car and would have liked to make conversation with her, but couldn't think of anything to say.

'Did you make a date with her?' Davy asked Parker when he came back in.

24

Spa Johnson phoned Parker in the evening. He said, 'There's something here you got to see.'

He didn't say where he was calling from, but in the background Parker could hear loud music.

'What's it about?' Parker asked.

'A Versace dress,' Spa said. 'I see a girl right here now in a Versace dress.'

'And where's that?'

'In Codere's Grove Wine and Dine.'

'I'll be there,' Parker said.

Codere's Grove was a ramshackle old wooden place on the low-rent side of the lake where the most fun was supposed to be, or at least where the most noise was made. Parker went in and it was plenty noisy and crowded.

He stood at the bar and, being tall, he could see over the heads to the dance floor, but he couldn't see a girl in a Versace dress. In fact, there were very few girls in any sort of dresses. A few wore skirts, but mostly they wore shorts and some were still in their bathing suits.

Parker remembered a vague time when they used to do Polish polka dancing at Codere's Grove. He had gone there often. There was a Polish girl that he fancied. In those days, Parker could almost play the saxophone and several times he had been called upon to play in Fred Skypeck's Polish polka band when the regular saxophonist was ill. The singer, he remembered, was a kid who didn't know any Polish and had to sing the songs reading the Polish words off the sheet music. Times, Parker thought, had been wonderfully amateurish then. The band playing now seemed too professional, and the scene being acted out in front of him could be almost anywhere. Back in the old days when Parker sometimes played in the Polish polka band there had been something especially local about it. The boys back then wore coats and ties and the girls were in dresses. 'Gosh,' Parker said to himself, 'we were in period costume then, only we didn't know it.' He saw himself then as if posing for a tin-type. 'It was more than a hundred years ago,' he told himself.

He went back to searching for the girl in the Versace dress.

There were booths round the dance floor. They had lattice-work round them and it was difficult to see who was sitting inside. Parker gave up looking for the Versace dress, which he thought he wouldn't be able to recognise, and tried to find Spa. Parker made his way round the dance floor, looking at the dancers and glancing into the booths. He felt an awful lot like a policeman, which made a change. He knew he must be terribly conspicuous. It was his age now and not his height that he thought made him stand out.

But no one was paying any attention to him. He might have been a ghost, the way they were looking right through him. A ghost would feel this way, he thought, if he came back to the house where he used to live and found strangers being right at home in all the rooms.

There was a hand on Parker's arm. It was Spa.

'I saw you,' Spa said. 'Right across the room. I followed your gumshoe progress sleuthing out the folk in the booths. I waved, but you didn't see. I called, but you didn't hear. She's over there, standing upside the wall by the door.'

Spa was dressed up rather sharp, as if he had put in a special order to Elroy Green or someone like Elroy Green to steal him some outstanding clothes.

Parker turned. The girl in the Versace dress was standing alone by the doorway where Parker had come in. There was no mistaking the dress. There was much skin showing, and Parker could see the bruises on her bare arms and on the one leg where it showed through a slit in the skirt. The girl moved her head and he could see that there was something odd about the way her face was made up. The colour around one eye was heavier than the other. Parker thought she might be trying to disguise a black eye.

'Let's go and grill her,' Spa said.

He turned and went up to the girl, walking ahead of Parker with quick, purposeful strides through the dancers. Wherever Spa had got the trousers they fell a little short in the leg, and there was a red gleam of flashy socks.

The girl in the Versace dress saw Spa and Parker coming, but she didn't try to get away.

She knew Spa, and she knew Parker was a cop. 'You under arrest again, Spa?' she asked.

She tried to smile but it evidently hurt her face and she stopped.

'No,' Spa said, 'but you soon might be. Mr Boomer Daniels, the chief, he's interested in that dress you're almost wearing.'

'Is he?' the girl said, looking Parker up and down, taking in the frayed collar of his shirt and the old trousers. 'He don't look like a fashion-conscious person,' she said.

Parker saw where the girl had been punched in the eye. It gave her face a lop-sided look.

'Oh, he's interested in ladies' apparel all right,' Spa said. He stood close to the girl, looking her up and down. She didn't seem to mind. 'He's especially interested in ladies' apparel that comes from a room that had a strangled man in it.'

The girl became concerned now. Her eyes darted around the room as though looking for someone to come and rescue her.

She spoke to Parker for the first time now. 'I didn't have nothing to do with that,' she said.

'We can't talk here,' Parker said. 'We can't stand here shouting about murder over the sound of this music.'

'Downtown?' Spa asked.

'No, no,' Parker said, 'there's no reason to take anyone to the station. Not yet at least.'

He was looking at the girl. He supposed the Versace dress was very expensive and very well-made, but she looked pathetic in it, like a child wearing her mother's clothes.

'We'll go outside,' Parker said. 'Onto the porch.'

Spa took the girl's arm like he was a gentleman escorting a lady and they went to the door. Spa's socks flashed the fancy red pattern and the girl's bare back and shoulders looked good, except for the bruises.

Codere's Grove had a wooden veranda that looked over the lake. There was some light out on the water but not much. The whites of Spa Johnson's eyes looked big in the dark. The girl's skin, which the famous dress didn't cover, glowed like pearl.

Parker thought he should be questioning the girl in a well-lighted room to see her face and tell if she was lying, but then he thought that he had never been very successful telling if a woman was lying to him, even when he was looking right at her with all the lights on.

Across the water Parker could see the lights of the amusement park. Every now and then he heard the sound of people squealing as they rode the machines. The roller-coaster appeared above the trees. People were screeching as they reached the top and then went suddenly wooshing down.

'Where'd you get that dress?' he asked.

'You know where she got it,' Spa said. 'That's not a very hard question.'

'I want to hear her answer it.'

'Elroy Green gave it to me,' she said.

'You didn't just happen to take it off him after you strangled him?' Spa said.

In the dark, not being able to see Spa's face, Parker had the idea that he was listening to Davy Shea questioning the girl. But perhaps that wasn't surprising. Spa had been stopped and questioned by a lot of police. He knew the way they talked. Besides, he was someone who sometimes thought he wanted to be an actor.

'I'll ask the questions,' Parker said, 'I'm the one the mayor made a policeman.'

The girl didn't seem any more pleased to be questioned by Parker.

'He gave me the dress,' she said. 'He came round to my place in Old Compton and he said, "Here you are, Louise, I hope this makes up for the trouble we had." I said, "Nothing is going to make up for that, you bastard." But I took the dress. I didn't know what it was. And then later on that day I heard that Elroy was dead.'

Parker's eyes had become accustomed to the half-light on the veranda. He could see the girl's face quite clearly looking up at him as she spoke. She seemed sincere, but there was something theatrical about the reflected lights from the amusement park and the expensive dress she was wearing.

'What trouble had Elroy Green given you?' Parker asked.

'He beat up on me,' she said. 'I only started going with him because Billy Zoots was beating up on me, but then Elroy was beating up on me too.'

'You were the girlfriend of them both?' Parker said.

'I wasn't the girlfriend of anyone,' she said, 'especially not of those two.'

'But he gave you the dress?' Parker said. 'He came to you straight from stealing it and gave it to you.'

'I told you. He was trying to get around me. After what he done, I wouldn't let him. I'd had enough. First Billy Zoots and then him.'

'That doesn't sound like Elroy Green,' Spa said, 'Elroy was too cool a guy to beat up on a woman.'

'That's what you know,' the girl said. 'Men, they never

106

know about other men and how handy they can be with their fists when a woman annoys them.'

'And Billy Zoots?' Spa said. 'I always thought he was too dumb to take offence.'

'He was worse,' she said, 'he was too thick in the head to be verbal when caught in an argument. He had no repartee, he had to hit.'

She seemed slightly bored now that she had told her story, which did not concern the dress or the murders, but was about how she was a woman who had been hit by men.

'I didn't kill no one,' she said, 'if that's what you were thinking. Do you think I'd kill Elroy Green for a dress, and then go out wearing it?'

'What else would you do with the dress but wear it?' Spa said.

Parker didn't say anything. He kept looking at her. 'Is this it?' he said to himself, 'Is this all there is?' He was wondering if the girl could have killed both Billy Zoots and Elroy Green. The knife in Billy Zoots' throat – anyone could have done that, the killer wouldn't have had to be strong. But the cord round Elroy Green's neck, that was something else. That took strength. But who was to say the girl didn't have it, especially if she was in a rage? A girl could get behind Elroy Green and slip the cord round his neck before he knew what she was doing. Estelle Ritter had seen a woman come to the house. Estelle had said something about the woman looking like she had a man who hit her, but Estelle hadn't mentioned bruises. The woman had said she was looking for Maria Esperanza, but if she was coming to kill Elroy Green she might say that; and the bruises she had now might have come from Elroy struggling. But Estelle said the woman was a blonde, this girl had dark hair. Still, there were wigs.

'What's your full name and address?' Parker asked. 'We might have to see you again. And we'll have to have the dress back, it's evidence.'

Her name was Louise Leclerc and she lived at Homestead Avenue in Old Compton. She didn't seem worried about him taking her name and address and she said she wasn't troubled about giving the dress back. 'I feel a fool in it anyway,' she said, 'where am I going to go in an outfit like this? I don't get invited to stuck-up places.'

'You come in tomorrow and leave the dress at the station,' Parker said.

'I don't know about tomorrow,' she said, 'I haven't got no one to look after my baby tomorrow.'

It seemed incredible to Parker that this girl, with her complicated love life and the bruises to prove it, had a child.

'Lou,' a voice said in the dark, 'I've been looking all over for you.'

Parker turned and saw a young man standing in the light from the open door.

'I'm here,' the girl said.

'I can see that,' the man said.

'I'll be going along now,' she said to Parker.

'Who's that?' Spa asked her.

'That's Dean Judd,' she said, 'he's been away, but he's back now.'

'Is that Dean Judd?' Spa said. 'I haven't seen him in years.'

'Are you coming?' Dean Judd asked her.

He was good-looking, but not as good-looking as Spa. Dean Judd wouldn't think of himself having movie star potential like Spa, and he wasn't dressed in expensive clothes. He looked shabby and poor.

'I got to go now,' Louise said to Parker.

'I'm waiting,' Dean Judd said.

The girl walked over to him.

'You look like hell,' Dean Judd said to her. 'That crazy dress, it looks like hell on you.'

They went back inside. Parker went to the car park.

Before he got into the old DeSoto, he stood watching the lights from the rollercoaster. He didn't like heights and he didn't like rollercoasters. But a lot of people did, they got a thrill out of the danger. He wondered if a girl like Louise Leclerc got the same sort of thrill being with dangerous men.

25

The next morning, sitting in the station, Parker remembered Kimberly Naundorff calling her daughter a has-been who hadn't made a movie in years. And yet Sally Sallas and Jack Coolidge had followed Julia Naundorff three thousand miles across the country to offer her a part.

Parker looked at the second designer dress that had been stolen from the house in Old Compton. He had heard of Versace, but he had never heard of Fortuny. He couldn't tell if it was old and out of fashion or the very latest thing. Ann West had said it was a collector's piece, worth a lot of money.

He telephoned Phyllis Skypeck and asked her to drop by the station whenever she had some free time, and then he phoned the Lake House Hotel and asked for Jack Coolidge. Parker had an idea that Coolidge might be more honest about Julia Naundorff's position in the movie world than Sallas would be.

Coolidge said he was coming into North Holford town centre to buy fish bait and that he'd come to the station. He didn't sound like a man who thought of himself as a suspect in a murder case.

Then Parker telephoned Estelle Ritter. She couldn't remember if the woman who came to the house on the day Elroy Green was murdered had bruises. She thought Parker was very odd, asking a question like that.

'Most women,' she said, 'got some bruises most of the time. They knock against things, not always men.'

When he put the phone down, Parker thought he should talk to Maria Esperanza again.

While the phone was ringing, Davy Shea said, 'Are you asking her to drop round too?'

Parker could tell Davy wouldn't mind seeing the curvy Maria Esperanza again. She had made an impression on Davy, and on young Georgie Stover too. They hadn't been able to take their eyes off her when she walked across the station floor.

When Maria Esperanza finally answered the phone she seemed out of breath. For a moment Parker thought maybe something awful had happened and he might have another corpse on his hands.

But she said she'd been downstairs when the phone rang and she had to run to answer it. Parker imagined her standing with the phone in her hand with a heaving bosom, trying to catch her breath. It was a sexy image, with that Latin face and the maroon lips and startling blonde hair.

'I'm calling,' Parker said, 'because I'm wondering if you've been able to recall anything more about the man you saw in the backyard.'

She said, 'When can I move into the room downstairs?'

'You're serious about that?'

'Of course.'

'Because of the vibrations?'

Parker thought he heard her laugh. It was all a con, he thought, the business of reading the cards and being clairvoyant and seeing auras round people's heads. Naturally sometimes she would have to laugh about the way she was taking the suckers in.

'It's on the ground floor,' she said, 'it's much better for business if people don't have to climb upstairs when they come to see me.'

Parker smiled. That was easier to understand than the

story about picking up vibrations from the departed spirit of Elroy Green. Still, the idea of connecting with the murdered man's ghost was nice and spooky and probably good for business.

'I'll see what I can do,' he said. Then he had a worrying thought about Maria Esperanza. She had startling blonde hair, like the three victims. Davy Shea had wondered if they were up against a crazed serial killer. Parker wondered if Davy could be right.

The room on the ground floor was more dangerous than the upstairs rooms where Maria Esperanza was living. A killer had already shown how easy it was to get into that ground-floor room and commit murder.

'I'll let you know when you can move. It'll be soon. Maybe tomorrow.'

They had got Elroy Green's belongings out of Liberty Street and the room had been dusted for prints. It was ready to be occupied by someone else.

'What about the man you saw in the backyard?' he asked.

'Nothing has come back to me,' Maria Esperanza said. 'Maybe when I'm living in his room, I'll see something.'

That wasn't what Parker was looking for. All he wanted was a good description of the man in the backyard. He couldn't see visions from the 'other side' standing up in court, no matter how often Maria Esperanza crossed her legs and heaved her bosom at the jury.

There was something else worrying him. He was beginning to grow suspicious of her. She was too keen to move into Elroy Green's rooms. He knew nothing about the woman except that she was good-looking and in the phony spook business. Those looks and the amusement he got out of the spook business had distracted him. She was a suspect too. She could have killed Elroy Green. She was big and strong enough, and with her looks she could have caught him off guard long enough to put the cord around his neck. A woman might have tied that fancy knot.

When Parker put the phone down, he said to Davy, 'We haven't taken up the floorboards in Liberty Street.'

'Elroy Green didn't make no attempt to hide anything,' Davy said. 'All that stolen stuff was right there out in the open.'

Parker said, 'I'm thinking we don't know anything about her, except that when she walks across a room, she's so dramatic that everyone has to look at her. There might be some other reason, other than vibrations and clients not having to walk upstairs, for her wanting to move into Elroy Green's old room. Get the floorboards up. And check the walls. See if there's a hollow wall.'

'Jesus, Boomer,' Davy said, 'that'll be a load of work.'

'Do it,' Parker said. 'Take Bob Vanderland with you, he'll like ripping up floorboards.'

Vanderland was a college kid working as a cop for a summer job. He was a rich college kid, his parents had a summer house on the lake and the mayor had been doing them a favour putting the kid on the force part-time. Vanderland was big and could handle himself in a fight, but the trouble was he started fights when they weren't necessary. Also he carried a gun just like a full-time cop, and although he hadn't used it, Parker could see he was keen to shoot someone, maybe almost as keen as Davy.

'Take Vanderland,' Parker said, 'and keep him from shooting anyone. I can't let you have Georgie, there's a big Red Sox game with the Yankees on TV and Georgie has to sit here and watch that.'

'What are we supposed to be looking for under the floorboards?' Davy asked.

'I don't know,' Parker said. 'I haven't the slightest idea.'

'That narrows it down,' Davy said.

A short time after he left, Phyllis arrived. She had come from the hospital in Holford, but she looked dressed for hiking in the woods, in a pair of old jeans and a checked shirt that looked like a lumberjack's summer wear. She also had on big boots that clumped across the floor. She looked the last girl you'd ask about *haute couture*.

She had diagnosed the expression on his face. 'You're thinking I don't look much like a medico,' she said. 'I've got a white coat in the car.'

He'd seen her at the hospital in the white coat.

She said, 'They trust me when they see the white coat. Of course the ones you've been bringing me to see are past worrying.'

'There has been an embarrassment of corpses,' Parker said.

'I like delivering babies,' Phyllis said. 'That's what I like best. I don't want any babies of my own, but if anyone bothered to ask me what I like the best, it's bringing in new babies. With the rest of it sometimes I think I'm working in a junkyard. With your stuff I feel that especially.'

'Is this junk?'

Parker went across the room and picked up the other designer dress that had been stolen from Julia Naundorff's room.

'Are you kidding?' Phyllis said.

She held the dress up to her as if seeing if it would fit her. It wouldn't. She was small and cute and Julia Naundorff had been big and dramatic.

'I've never had anything like this,' Phyllis said. 'In fact I've never seen anything like this except in magazines, very expensive magazines.'

'It's worth a lot of money then?'

'You bet.'

She told him about Fortuny.

She examined it some more. Parker couldn't imagine himself getting that much pleasure out of any clothing. He thought they must make a strange picture, the girl dressed like she'd just come in from the logging camp and him, in his shirt with the frayed collar and his high-water trousers, looking over a Fortuny dress that came from

Paris in the 1920s and must have cost as much as a new car.

'I've seen this dress before,' Phyllis said.

'You have?'

'I don't mean I've met it socially. I've never been anywhere where a dress like this would be. I mean I've seen it in a magazine.'

'I can't see how people could bring themselves to spend that kind of money,' Parker said.

'You wouldn't,' she said, still admiring the dress. 'You're sure of yourself, you're right at home in your skin.'

'I am?'

The idea was news to Parker. He always felt he was too tall and awkward.

'Sure you are,' she said, still studying the dress, not bothering to look at him.

Just then the outside door of the station opened and Jack Coolidge walked in.

He was wearing old jeans and a checked shirt, also heavy boots. He and Phyllis looked as if they might have been twins, except Coolidge was older.

'Hello,' he said. He was addressing Phyllis. She smiled at him.

'I'm not a cop,' she said. 'Boomer's the cop.' She turned to Parker. 'Is that all?' she asked.

'Yeah,' Parker said.

'I'll let you know if I remember where I saw the dress,' she said. She looked at Coolidge again, then turned and walked to the door.

Coolidge watched her leave.

26

'A nice girl,' Coolidge said. 'A fine-looking woman.'

The remark seemed a bit old-fashioned after the way Coolidge had been ogling Phyllis in her tight-fitting jeans.

But Phyllis had also been looking at Coolidge. She was a single girl and unattached and Coolidge was a handsome guy who looked good dressed up as a fisherman, although Parker thought he wasn't really the outdoor type, more like an actor in the role of a rugged guy who went fishing.

Parker looked at Coolidge's hands. They weren't manicured, but they were soft, the hands of a man who spent his time inside doing paperwork. That was all right. It was only proper. Coolidge was supposed to be a Hollywood writer. That was the role he played for money in the real world.

'What can I do for you?' he asked Parker.

Coolidge was at ease. Parker could see he wasn't bothered about being in a police station. He kept looking around the station as though he might use it in a story sometime. Parker thought the hick station mustn't look too impressive, and not at all menacing.

'Have you figured out yet what time you saw Julia Naundorff go in the water?' Parker asked.

'I thought it was early. When we first got out on the lake, but Sal, he says it was a long time after that.'

'Neither of you are sure?'

'I'm afraid not. Is it important?'

'I suppose not. We've got witnesses who saw her driving her car, and they remember when that was.'

'Is that all you wanted to see me about?'

'Did you know Julia Naundorff well?'

'Not really. She was a friend of Sal's. Sal took me to

meet her. He had an idea she'd be good in a part in a script I'd done.'

'A big part?'

'No, as a matter of fact, a small one,' Coolidge said.

'A cameo?'

Coolidge smiled. Parker imagined the Hollywood writer was amused by the hick cop using a theatrical term.

'Yes,' Coolidge said. 'I wasn't sure she'd be right for it. But Sal was convinced.'

'It seems you two went to a lot of trouble coming all the way out here to see her about it.'

'That was Sal again. I didn't mind. I wanted a break. And it would be good if we could get her to make a comeback in such an unusual role for her.'

'A comeback?'

'Yeah, sure. She hadn't been in anything for some time.'

Coolidge spoke as if the whole world knew about Julia Naundorff and it was surprising that Parker didn't know.

'What happened to her?' Parker asked.

'She got old.'

'Did she?'

She hadn't seemed old to Parker, but he had only ever seen her dead in the water, dead on the canvas covering of the boatdock, and dead again in a mortuary. They weren't flattering settings, but she hadn't looked old, and she wasn't going to get any older.

'For the type of actress she was,' Coolidge said, 'for the parts she played, she was too old. Don't you know her stuff? I thought everyone had seen at least some of her movies.'

'No,' Parker said, 'I never go to the movies any more.'

'They're shown on TV,' Coolidge said.

'I don't watch much TV,' Parker said, and he almost added that his TV was broken, except he had an idea it might make him seem awful sad.

'You ought to get some DVDs and see her. She was very good, for the type she was.'

Parker thought they were getting away from the subject, which was Julia dead. 'After a death like hers,' he said, 'it's interesting to see who'll benefit.'

'You're still thinking of that reincarnation guy.'

'He admits he was there, he says he didn't see anything. But he's got a motive.'

'Has he?'

'He's going to get Julia Naundorff's money.'

'I don't think you've got much of a motive there,' Coolidge said. 'The family is bound to contest the will and they'll probably win.'

Parker couldn't see Ann West contesting the will. She at least was getting the farm. But there was Kimberly Naundorff, the mother, she'd contest the will all right.

Parker thought of Spendlove in his cleaned and pressed suit and shiny shoes, sitting in the lounge at the College Inn, ordering dry martinis and behaving like a man who'd just won the lottery.

'Tell me again,' Parker said, 'about seeing Julia Naundorff going into the water.'

Coolidge didn't seem to mind. He told the story better this time, at least he worked in more atmosphere. Parker could see handsome Jack Coolidge and the little fat man out in the boat on the lake with the sun coming through the haze and the water still as a plate, and Coolidge turning and seeing the woman on the boatdock. She stood for a moment and then she fell and Coolidge turned away because he thought he had a fish on his line.

'The wind,' Parker said, 'you forgot the wind this time. The first time you told it, the wind was quite poetic. You should try to remember everything. But if there wasn't anyone near Julia Naundorff on shore, we're left with only you and Sallas in the boat.'

For the first time Parker spoke in an aggressive manner. Coolidge was aware of the change.

'Listen,' he said, 'I didn't do anything.'

117

'You mean Sallas did?'

'No, no, neither of us.'

Coolidge wasn't so smooth now. He looked like he was about to break out in a sweat. The door of the station opened and Phyllis Skypeck came in. Parker saw that Coolidge wasn't looking at her this time, not the way he had looked at her before. Parker supposed that was a proper response for a man who had just become a murder suspect.

27

'Can I talk here, Boomer?' Phyllis asked. She glanced at Coolidge.

'Is it about the case?' Parker said.

'I guess it is,' she said.

'Mr Coolidge is just leaving,' Parker said.

Coolidge got to his feet. He was looking at Phyllis again now and she was pretending not to notice.

When Coolidge left Phyllis said, 'I told you that dress looked familiar. Then I found this.'

She had a glossy magazine. It was folded back to a spread about a party in Hollywood. 'OSCAR NIGHT AT SAL'S' was the headline.

Sally Sallas was apparently famous for the parties he threw after the Oscars were awarded. Parker recognised the little fat man, looking little and fat, but younger.

'It's a long time ago,' Phyllis said.

Parker looked at the date on the magazine. It was from ten years ago. Phyllis was obviously a girl with longings for glamour and riches, keeping a magazine like that. It wasn't unusual, but he hadn't thought she was like that.

'There's the dress,' she said.

Her finger pointed to a woman on the page.

Parker didn't recognise the dress. Or the woman wearing it. But there was a caption underneath. It said the woman was Julia Naundorff and the dress she was wearing was an original Fortuny from the 1920s.

Julia Naundorff was also wearing something else. She was holding onto a young guy like he was the latest fashion accessory.

'Look at that,' Phyllis said, pointing to the caption.

The guy in the picture was Jack Coolidge and Julia Naundorff had a grip on him as if she knew him very well or was soon going to.

28

Davy and Vanderland came back from the Ritter house on Liberty Street. They hadn't found anything under the floorboards but dust. Vanderland was in a sharp new uniform and he didn't like having it dirty. He liked looking sharp for the girls he met out on patrol by the big public beach at Black Point. Outside of getting to shoot someone, Vanderland was mainly interested in girls. He kept trying to brush the dirt off his shirt and pants.

'Go home and change,' Parker said, 'if it bothers you that much.' He didn't like Vanderland, but when half a dozen cops had been dismissed on corruption charges, Parker had to take what he could get.

'What about me?' Davy said. He was dusty too.

'On you it looks good,' Parker said. 'So there was nothing there?'

'Not a thing. And Estelle Ritter went spare having her floor torn up. And Maria Esperanza wasn't too pleased either since she's going to move in there.'

'I had to do it,' Parker said.

'You?' Davy said. 'You had to do it?' He looked down at his dusty clothes.

'I mean eliminate Maria Esperanza as a suspect. She's the one who must have seen Elroy Green's killer and it wouldn't be very good if we couldn't trust her because we thought she might have done it herself.'

'I don't know how much of a willing police witness she's going to be after what we done to her room,' Davy said.

'I think she's a woman who's used to cops being tough with her,' Parker said.

'So who are the other suspects?' Davy said. 'And do they have floors to tear up?'

'The list of suspects has grown.' Parker told Davy about Jack Coolidge lying to him about knowing Julia Naundorff.

'I figure it's that Englishman,' Davy said.

'Spendlove isn't English,' Parker said.

'Well, he's something like that. Anyway, he's the one with the motive.' Then he added, 'It's a difficult one, that Naundorff killing. The others are easier.'

'Are they?' Parker said. 'I don't see what's so easy about them.'

'Well,' Davy said, 'I guess it's pretty clear that Elroy Green killed Billy Zoots.'

'Is it?' Parker said. 'Or does it only look that way? And Elroy Green can't tell us anything because unfortunately someone killed him.'

'Your private investigator Spa Johnson hasn't come up with anything on that,' Davy said.

'He found the Versace dress,' Parker said, 'and a girl in it.'

'That don't clear anything up,' Davy said.

He was right. Parker had to agree with him. Finding Louise Leclerc in the stolen dress had only added another suspect. Two other suspects. Louise Leclerc had that boyfriend Dean Judd and from what Parker saw of him he had looked like the kind of small-town tough guy who might get ambitious and turn his hand to murder.

'What do we know about Dean Judd?' Parker asked.

Davy shrugged. 'He's a small-change punk.'

'Could he kill anyone?'

'I suppose so,' Davy said, 'if the mood stole over him.'

'Billy Zoots and Elroy Green beat up on Louise Leclerc,' Parker said. 'Maybe Dean Judd got chivalrous.'

Davy started to laugh and then he saw Parker wasn't trying to be funny.

Parker said, 'Louise Leclerc seems to have forgot about handing in that Versace dress. I guess I better go to Old Compton and get it.'

'There's another suspect in Old Compton that you're forgetting,' Davy said.

'She's got an alibi,' Parker said. 'She was out shopping when her stepsister went into the lake.'

'We've only got that guy Coolidge's word for that,' Davy said. 'Maybe her and Coolidge are in it together.'

'How could they be? She doesn't know Coolidge.'

'Who's word do you have for that?' Davy said.

29

Parker took the car ferry across the lake. It was still light and there were plenty of people swimming and many boats on the water. In the country lanes on the other side the traffic was slow because of a farmer's tractor pulling a wagon piled high with hay. The tourists were impatient being held up behind this, but the road was too narrow for them to pass. When the farmer on the tractor pulled off the road the traffic speeded up, but then a flock of sheep

121

appeared in the road. Some of the tourists got impatient, but others watched the sheep and looked pleased about it because this was what they had come to the country to see. There was a man with two young boys and a border collie driving the sheep, and up ahead, leading the flock, Parker saw the blonde head of Ann West. She looked completely countrified. No one seeing her could imagine that she was the sister of a famous movie star.

There was a convertible with the top down stopped in the traffic in front of Parker. The passengers got out to watch the sheep as the driver inched the car forward. Ann's farmhouse appeared in the distance and one of the women pointed to it. Parker knew they were saying that was the house where the movie star had lived or, if they didn't know about that, maybe they were saying what a good place it looked to live, with the heaviest traffic outside only sheep being moved from one field to another.

Ann led the sheep into a field and the tourists got back into the convertible and the traffic moved quickly on. Parker tried to get a look at Ann when he drove by, but she was already out of sight.

Homestead Avenue was farther on. There used to be farms there, but it had become a street of run-down houses. At one time there had been talk of trying to remove the poor people from the houses and turning it into a tourist attraction. It had historic interest, a famous Indian attack had taken place there in the eighteenth century. A small brook, very old and twisted like ribbon candy, ran behind Homestead Avenue and it was said to have run red with blood, warning the settlements far downstream that there had been a massacre.

Parker couldn't imagine what sort of theme park or museum that would make. It was hard now, driving past the pathetic houses, to visualise Indians coming out of the woods and across the cornfields to kill the settlers. But then he thought that the houses of the early settlers wouldn't have been any more substantial than the ones here now, and that the settlers were probably even more poor and shabby-looking than the present residents of Homestead Avenue.

He found Louise Leclerc's house. It was wooden and it needed paint. There was an old car out front that looked like it hadn't been driven in a long time. Still, Parker thought, it didn't look much worse than his own old DeSoto.

The steps up to the porch were broken and the porch itself didn't seem too safe. There was a screen door with half the screening rusted away. The inner door was open but the little hallway was dark. Parker pressed the bell but it didn't ring. He knocked but it seemed a feeble summons. For a moment he had a dreadful feeling that there would be another dead body inside.

But then he heard the sound of feet and a woman appeared. He wondered who she was, then she said, 'Oh, it's you. I thought it might be Dean coming back and being polite knocking at the door.'

Louise Leclerc looked worn out. Parker thought she might be ill, then he saw that she wasn't wearing any make-up. The swelling round her eye had gone down but both eyes looked sore. The lids were red and the eyes looked naked. Her face was pale and her hair was set flat about her head as if she had been wearing a cap. She wore a man's shirt that was almost as old and frayed and wrinkled as his own. It hung down and made it seem as if she wasn't wearing anything else until he saw the ragged edge of jeans that had been cut down to make shorts.

'I look a mess,' she said.

She clutched the front of the shirt as if she might be offending modesty.

'No, no,' Parker said, 'you look perfectly all right.'

He was thinking she looked like one of the pioneer women who had been here when the Redmen attacked. She was French and the French were the settlers here too, along with the old Yankees. A face like that would have looked out over the cornfields and seen the half-naked figures moving out from under the trees and then whooping through the green stalks of the cornfield. He imagined the woman clutching a child to her, and on cue a small child came crawling out from a room and put its arms round Louise Leclerc's legs. The mother bent down and picked it up, completing his vision. Except Louise Leclerc's bare legs were wrong, and the child wore a T-shirt with a picture of a cartoon character on it.

'I thought you were Dean,' Louise said again. 'You'll want the dress. That was a mistake. It didn't fit. It wasn't right anyway. Not for someone like me. Dean, he laughed at me for wearing it. Then we had a fight and he left. I hope for good.'

She led Parker into the front room. It was dark. The shades were pulled down halfway. There wasn't much furniture, and what was there was cheap, but there was a desk in the corner with a new computer on it.

She saw him taking it in.

'I work here, it's not stolen,' she said. 'It's mine, I've got the bill for it. I do work at home.'

Still holding the child she reached over and took a piece of paper from the desk. It had the name of a local insurance agent printed at the top.

'I used to work there,' she said. 'In the office,' she added as though that gave her status. 'When I couldn't any more on account of Simone he gave me work to do at home, writing to prospectives. Harvey Alderman, he's been good to me, plus he got some others to give me work, but it's beginning to dry up.'

'You were Harvey Alderman's secretary?'

'Sure, but more like the general office manager. I did all the filing. Harvey, he gave me the money for this computer. I can do colour printing.'

Parker was wondering who he knew who could give her some work.

She put the child down.

'I'll get the dress,' she said.

When she came downstairs with the dress, she had put on a baggy sweater.

'Here,' she said. She had folded the dress and shoved it into a plastic shopping bag.

Parker was going to ask her about Dean Judd, but she didn't seem in the mood to answer questions. He stood holding the plastic bag with the expensive dress crammed into it and he knew he must be looking particularly stupid.

'Well?' the woman said.

'Dean Judd,' Parker said, 'he must have been pretty upset about Billy Zoots and Elroy Green beating up on you.'

'Why? Because he thought that was his job? What do you want now? You got the dress. What are you doing standing there looking down at me?'

Parker didn't know what to say. He didn't like the idea of the child being in the room when he was talking of murder.

'Oh, I see,' the woman said, 'you're thinking of pinning those murders on Dean. Jesus, you cops. Someone told me you weren't a real cop, but you're a real cop all right.'

'What's going on?' a man said.

Parker turned. Dean Judd was there. Parker hadn't heard him come in.

Louise said, 'It's just Boomer Daniels trying to pin a couple of murder raps on you.'

'Say,' Dean said to Parker, 'is my cousin working for you?'

'Your cousin?'

'Yeah, Spa Johnson, my cousin.'

Spa lied to me, Parker thought, he pretended he didn't know Dean Judd well at all. Perhaps it's understandable, with a cousin like Dean Judd. There was no family resemblance, except they were both good-looking. But Dean had the mark of defeat on him. He lacked the humour and vitality that Spa had. He was worn out and defeated, like the woman with the child, which might or might not be his.

'He's been helping me,' Parker said of Spa.

Dean was no longer interested. He spoke to the woman.

'I been down to Dime's garage, but he didn't have the spare parts I wanted. I picked up a good distributor cap, though.' He held the distributor cap up to show her. Then he put it down on the desk.

'Not there,' she said, 'it'll get the paper all greasy. What are you doing here anyway? This is my house, not yours.'

'I rescued you from Elroy Green.'

'Yeah, sure, and Elroy rescued me from Billy Zoots. I'm so grateful to have had so many rescuing men in my life. It seems to me I wouldn't need rescuing if all you men would go away.' Then she said to Parker, 'Go ahead, ask him about Billy Zoots and Elroy Green.'

'What's this about Billy Zoots and Elroy Green?' Dean asked. 'Let him ask away, I've got nothing to hide.'

'He'll want to know where you were when Billy Zoots got his throat stabbed and when Elroy Green got himself strangled. I'd like to know where you were too. That's something that would interest me, because you certainly weren't with me.'

'She thinks I was off seeing another woman,' Dean said.

He looked at Parker, seeking understanding. Dean wasn't very big, but he was wiry. Parker was trying to imagine him coming at Billy Zoots with a knife. He could see that, but it was harder to imagine him tackling Elroy Green who was big and had looked strong even dead with the cord tied round his neck with the fancy knot.

Dean spoke to the woman.

'I told you,' he said, 'I was looking for work. I was in Holford seeing about a bus-driving job when Billy Zoots was killed. I don't know when Elroy was killed. If you tell me what time that was, I'll tell you what I was doing.'

'It was late Tuesday afternoon,' Parker said.

He didn't want to question the man here, but it seemed he had no choice.

'You got me there,' Dean said. 'I can't remember exactly where I was on Tuesday early evening. But it may come to me.'

'Yeah,' Louise said, 'when I'm not around you can sneak down to the police station and give him the name of the woman you were with.'

'That's not true,' Dean said.

'Isn't it?'

She picked up the child and went out of the room.

Dean walked to the door with Parker and then, after some hesitation, came outside and went with him to Parker's car.

He said, 'That time of day, on Tuesday when Elroy was killed, I remember it now where I was.'

'With a woman?'

'Yeah, that's true enough. But we went somewhere. We were seen.'

'Oh yeah?'

'Yeah, we went to score some dope.'

'You can give me a name?'

'Of the woman or where we went to score?'

'Both.'

'I don't like to do it,' Dean said.

He looked very concerned, but Parker couldn't tell if it was about giving the woman's name or informing about the dope peddler.

'The girl was Suzanne Leclerc,' Dean said, 'Louise's kid sister.'

'I see,' Parker said. 'And the man with the dope you went to see?'

'Your pal, my cousin Spa Johnson,' Dean said.

30

When Parker left Homestead Avenue he remembered Davy's sarcastic remark about another suspect in Old Compton.

There was no real reason for him to go to Ann West's. He should be going to see Spa to check on Dean Judd's story, and to warn Spa against selling dope. But that could wait.

He stood at the front door of Ann's house, ringing the bell. No one answered and he started to leave when he heard a dog barking.

A small girl came round the side of the house. She had the Staffordshire bull terrier pup on a lead.

'They're not here,' the girl said. 'They're in the orchard.'

She looked familiar, but he couldn't remember where he had seen her.

'This way,' she said.

She took Parker's hand. She was a solemn child of about eight. She was frowning, concentrating on the responsibility of leading both Parker and the pup.

'I don't know how smart it is for you to be so friendly with strangers,' Parker said.

'It's OK,' she said, 'you're a policeman. At least you're pretending to be one.'

Parker laughed. 'Who told you that?'

'My uncle. He didn't tell me, but I heard him tell someone.'

'So that's what they say about me?'

'Yes,' the child said with the serious look still on her face. She kept hold of his hand as though he were the village idiot and might run away and get lost.

They walked away from the house and down a lane to an orchard. Parker could see Ann and several men under the trees. They were cutting grass. There was an automatic Allen scythe with a stuttering engine that one of the men was operating, walking slowly behind it while two men raked the new cut grass into rows. Parker recognised one as the man who had brought the Staffordshire bull terrier pup to Ann, saying the dog made his wife nervous. Parker didn't know the other, and the man with the Allen scythe was too far away for him to see.

Ann had a pitchfork and was turning grass which had been cut earlier. It was already drying, at least on top, where it had been exposed to the sun. Where she turned it over, it was still bright green.

'Mr Daniels,' she said.

She stopped work and smiled at him. She was wearing a red headscarf that left only a bit of her yellow hair showing. Standing there with the pitchfork she looked like a nineteenth-century painting. Except her shirt was wet with sweat and had become transparent. It stuck to her skin and the nipples showed through. Parker could imagine that happening a lot in the nineteenth century before bras were invented, only they wouldn't show it in a painting of hay-making.

'Have you come to help?' she asked.

He didn't seem to have a choice.

She handed him the pitchfork and walked over to the shade of an apple tree and got herself another one. She was wearing lightweight khaki trousers and they stuck to her almost as much as the shirt did.

'We can't get the tractor in here with the big cutter or the baler because of the trees,' she said. 'We have to use that old Allen scythe. We have to do it the old-fashioned way by hand and build a rick.'

Parker followed her long grey eyes to a pile of hay at the top of the orchard some hundred yards away.

'The hay over there has been made,' she said. She pointed to rows piled up between the trees. 'It would be great if you could help bring it to the rick.

The man whose wife didn't like dogs lifted a load of hay on the end of his pitchfork. He walked towards the rick with the hay held over his head. The ball of hay seemed larger than him and yet he was able to pitch it up to the top of the rick, which was already quite high. A girl stood on top of the rick and caught the new hay, placing it at one corner, then tramping it down to make a firm edge.

Parker tried to fork the hay and carry it like the man did. As he staggered to the rick he could feel some of the hay slipping away. He felt very inept.

'What a load you've got,' Ann said. 'That's really impressive.'

Parker felt tremendously cheered. He pitched the hay up to the girl on the rick. He recognised her. He knew now where he had seen the little girl who had taken him by the hand and led him here. They were Whitey Gotton's nieces who had discovered Julia Naundorff's body in the water by the boatdock. The girl on the top of the rick was the oldest one. Parker saw now that the man following the automatic scythe through the long grass was Whitey Gotton.

Parker continued carrying hay to the rick. He was soaked with sweat and it got harder and harder to throw up the loads to the top of the growing stack, but he felt good and the hay had a marvellous smell.

As it grew dark the scene took on an unreal quality.

'It's getting too dark,' Ann said.

Parker had hay in his hair and down the back of his neck. He leaned on the pitchfork watching her. Ann and the children seemed perfectly at home in this world that was so strange to him.

She went to Whitey Gotton. He turned off the machine.

'The grass is getting wet again,' he told her. 'It's hard to cut. We'll finish tomorrow.'

130

'How's your arm?' she said. 'I wonder if you should be doing this with that shoulder of yours.'

'It's fine,' he said, 'it's OK.'

'It's very kind of you,' Ann said, 'I don't know what I'd have done without you.'

Whitey was collecting his nieces. The Staffordshire bull terrier came to Ann. The other men walked off, making an old-fashioned scene with their pitchforks in the fading light.

'I've really taken terrible advantage of you,' Ann said to Parker.

She still wore the headscarf and the strands of blonde hair that stuck out from under it looked very white and her face seemed to glow. It was the moonlight. A big harvest moon flooded the field so they had no trouble seeing.

'Are you doing anything?' she asked. 'If you're not going anywhere special, you must let me give you a drink. A real drink.'

Parker told himself that he should show her the dress and ask her about her sister's finances. That seemed excuse enough to stay for a drink.

Ann bent down, patting the dog.

'You've been a good girl, Moll,' she said.

She straightened up and looked across the orchard. 'Whitey,' she called to where he was standing with his nieces, 'will you have a drink?'

'I think I'd better get these girls home,' Whitey said.

'He's been so good,' Ann said to Parker. 'You know he's got that bad shoulder. That's why he does all that fishing, to strengthen it. But I don't think standing all day behind that old Allen scythe could be much good for it.'

Parker followed her and the dog out of the field and down into the lane that led back to the house.

'I'm sorry about dragooning you,' she said. 'It was very sporting of you to give it a try.'

'Was it so very obvious that I'm no good as a farmhand?'

'Not so very. I like hay-making. At least when you know it's not going to rain and you've brought it in. I suppose I should have music and dancing, like something out of Thomas Hardy. At least you and I'll have a drink.'

It was dark in the lane with the trees blocking the moonlight.

'Smell the hay,' she said, 'you can still smell it from here.'

They came out from under the trees and her house stood looking very pretty in the moonlight.

'Just a minute,' he said, 'I've got something to show you.'

He went to the car and brought the dress in the bag to her. He opened the bag and pulled the dress out.

'Is this it?' he asked.

'In this light I can't see.'

She held the dress up.

'It looks like it,' she said. 'Yes, this is it.'

Parker put it back in the bag.

'I'll have to keep it a while. It's evidence.'

He put it in the car.

When they came into the house Parker felt as if he hadn't really seen it before. He had been concentrating on the dead body of Billy Zoots and on the robbery in the house, also on the sight of Ann's long legs. He saw now that the house looked much more expensive than he had thought. There was still a shabbiness about it, but the antique furniture and carpets were the stuff of rich people. He felt out of place.

'She's another rich girl,' he said to himself.

Rich women were something to be avoided. He had been brought up that way, or perhaps it had been something he just knew and didn't have to be taught. Then, by mistake, he had met one and it didn't seem to matter and they had been married and then it did matter. Parker blamed himself. When the marriage was over, friends told him it wasn't his fault, but he still blamed himself. He had known that they wouldn't be right together, but he had put it out of his mind and had gone ahead with the romance. His friends smiled because Parker's rich wife had gone off with another working-class guy. Parker couldn't see how that made any difference to the mistake he had made.

Ann brought him a beer. He drank it standing up, like a yardman being given a treat in the kitchen.

'Why don't you sit down?' Ann said.

Parker was thinking of Kimberly Naundorff. She was an unusual stepmother for a girl like Ann to have. Kimberly must have come as a shock when Ann's father brought her home, a big Southern cracker with Julia, the performing kid, always singing and dancing.

'Your stepmother,' he said, 'she doesn't seem to know that your sister's money's going to Mr H. P. Spendlove.'

'I think she does,' Ann said, 'and I imagine she'll kick up about that and contest the will. She might not even like it that Julia left me the farm. Oh sit down,' she said. 'You make me nervous standing there, being so tall.'

Parker sat down.

'If you're here on business,' Ann said, 'you might as well talk about murder. Where did you find the dress?'

'A woman called Louise Leclerc had it. Elroy Green gave it to her. Or at least that's what she said.'

'How'd you ever find her?'

'A fellow who's doing some snooping around for me, he saw her in it.'

'That's incredible. You mean she actually wore it out somewhere?'

'To Codere's Grove. My man saw her there.'

'Your man? You mean that Spa character?'

'I guess I do,' Parker said.

'I want to hear about the case,' she said. 'I do. It's only natural that I'd be interested. Tell me about your spy.'

'Spa? There's not much to tell about Spa. I went to high school with his brother Edgar, he's a professor at BU now.'

'Is he? Is he really?'

She seemed to prefer Spa as a mysterious underworld character, not as a man with a college-professor brother. Parker told her about Spa pretending to be a Puerto Rican when he was trying to rob the liquor store.

She said, 'I hear you've also got a clairvoyant. Whitey heard that.'

Parker told her about Maria Esperanza.

'You've seen her,' he said, 'she was in the police station.'

'The glamour girl with the yellow hair and maroon lips?'

'That's right. It's not her special powers we want. She saw someone in the backyard at Liberty Street. I want a description from her.'

'Couldn't it have been very simple, couldn't this Elroy Green have killed both Billy Zoots and my sister and then some other unknown thief came to rob him?'

'I suppose it could be something like that. Davy Shea thinks it is, when he's not thinking it's a crazy man with a hatred of yellow hair. I suppose later on we'll catch a thief and he'll turn out to be our killer.'

'But you don't really think so?'

'No, the way your stepsister was killed was too clever. It's totally different from the murders of Zoots and Green.'

'Maybe they're not connected?'

'Oh, they're connected all right. I'm sure of that. The killer thought of a brilliant way to kill your stepsister, but he was interrupted by Billy Zoots and he had to get rid of Zoots, in a very unbrilliant way. He had to do the same with Elroy Green, but he was seen.'

'By the clairvoyant lady?'

'That's right.'

'Only she can't remember?'

'Not yet.'

Parker finished the beer. He stood up. 'I've got to go see Spa Johnson now.'

Ann was on her feet. They were standing close. Parker

wanted to look away, but he thought she would notice even more that way how nervous she made him.

She thanked him again for helping with the hay.

When he was outside walking to his car, he turned and looked back at the house. He could see her standing in the kitchen. The headscarf was off and her hair looked very blonde. She was talking on the telephone.

He stood looking at her yellow hair for a few moments and then he went away.

31

Spa Johnson had some news for Parker.

'I found out there was a man asking for Liberty Street. A spooky guy, in a hat and suit. Talked something like an Englishman.'

'H. P. Spendlove.'

'The same. Only he wasn't asking for Elroy Green. He was looking for Maria Esperanza, the fortune-teller.'

Parker thought he should go to the College Inn and see H. P. Spendlove sometime that day. He wanted to ask Spendlove why he had been looking for Maria Esperanza, a woman he said he couldn't remember having met.

Parker drove to the College Inn and when he came in he could see there was something odd because Kimberly Naundorff was standing there dressed as a waitress.

She was looking very big and blonde. She seemed at home and perfectly happy working as a waitress again.

'What are you doing working here?' Parker asked.

'Earning a living, what do you think?'

The big woman smiled. 'Say,' she said, 'you don't know, do you?'

'I guess I don't.'

'The news is this, chief,' she said, 'I've got to work, there isn't going to be any money from Julia.'

She sounded quite happy about it, as if she was re-assured about fate not producing any surprises and her luck proving bad again, just as it always was.

Parker said, 'I'm sorry about that. So Mr H. P. Spendlove is actually going to get it all?'

'Well,' she said, 'There isn't that much. Sal Sallas telephoned Julia's lawyer in LA and he broke the bad news.'

She smiled as if it were the very opposite of bad news, but there was something odd about her colourful speech. She was like an actress playing a big Southern momma. It was unreal.

She said, 'Right away I legged it down quick to see the management about figuring some way I could pay the hotel bill.'

Kimberly Naundorff smiled, and then suddenly frowned and looked serious.

'Are you going to catch the murderer, chief?'

'We're trying.'

Kimberly stood gazing at him as if she was studying his character.

'I think it would be a popular move if you arrested Spendlove,' she said. 'He's pretty unlikable.'

Parker knew what she meant. Spendlove looked a suspicious character.

Parker left her and went to find Spendlove.

Small-town prejudice in fact would be satisfied if H. P. Spendlove and Maria Esperanza were together in on the crimes. Maria Esperanza was another mysterious stranger. Parker wasn't sure which was the more exotic, a clairvoyant or a man who could remember past incarnations. Neither one was a thing people in the lake area went in for, not publicly when sober at least, and the fact of Spendlove and Maria Esperanza making money out of it was viewed with suspicion.

136

Estelle Ritter's rooming house down on Liberty Street was a curious place for Maria Esperanza to set up in business. Parker guessed she wasn't making much money. But perhaps she had come to North Holford for another reason. If she and Spendlove had come to town to murder Julia Naundorff, then Maria Esperanza might very well establish herself in Liberty Street. But wasn't it too much of a coincidence that Elroy Green would be living in the same house? And he was forgetting the woman in dark glasses whom Estelle Ritter said called.

He found Spendlove in the lounge.

Spendlove said, 'That fat Irish copper Shea came in here and questioned me at some length. At least, he kept asking me what I thought of yellow hair. Is he all right in the head?'

Parker sat down opposite Spendlove. This time Spendlove didn't offer him a drink, and the young waitress who had been dancing round Spendlove the other day wasn't dancing now. The word about the will has obviously got out, Parker thought.

There was something different about Spendlove and Parker couldn't see at first what it was, and then he saw that he was no longer in mourning. The black tie was replaced by a natty number, a floral arrangement that looked like it was being struck by lightning. The suit that Spendlove wore today was a light grey dove colour, summer weight. Even with the florid tie and lack of black, Spendlove still looked somehow sinister. Kimberly Naundorff had been right about him being a popular murder suspect. The newspaper photographers would love him. People seeing him would be comforted, thinking that murder was something done by recognisable types.

'And how do you feel about yellow hair?' Parker asked.

Spendlove grinned.

'I knew what Shea was up to,' he said. 'He wants there to be a maniac loose on the lake. It's a great story. But I wonder how much the mayor and the board of selectmen would like it? A maniac running loose, killing blondes of either sex wouldn't be too good for the tourist trade.'

Parker smiled in a polite way at Spendlove's joke.

'Where are you from, Mr Spendlove?'

'I've already told you, Ohio.'

'I've called that place in Ohio, there's no record of any Spendlove there.'

'There wouldn't be. Spendlove was my stepfather's name. I was born Smith.'

Parker was surprised. Spendlove didn't look ordinary enough ever to have been a Smith.

'Most people round here,' Parker said, 'think you're an Englishman.'

'My stepfather was.'

'Oh,' Parker said.

He wanted to bring up the subject of Maria Esperanza, but he didn't know how to do it.

'Mr Spendlove,' Parker said, 'you take a taxicab ride out to a house on the lake one morning and the next thing we know there's two dead people there. Then you go asking about a house on Liberty Street and then there's another dead body there.'

'You know about that?' Spendlove said.

He was no longer grinning.

'Know about what?' Parker asked.

'Liberty Street,' Spendlove said and he seemed suddenly sad as if some terrible weight had come down on his skinny shoulders.

'What do I know about Liberty Street?' Parker asked.

'She lives there,' Spendlove said, putting a lot of emphasis on the word she. He tried to smile, but he didn't seem to have the energy to produce a good one.

'You mean Miss Esperanza?'

'I mean Mrs Spendlove.'

Parker wondered if he had got something wrong and

there was another woman whom he hadn't heard about living at Estelle Ritter's house on Liberty Street.

'Maria Esperanza and I are married,' Spendlove said and it sounded like the saddest thing in the world. 'You see,' he said, 'she ran away from me.'

'You came to North Holford to see Julia Naundorff and you just happened to find that your runaway wife was living here?'

It seemed an unlikely coincidence to Parker.

'No, the other way around. I came here hunting for her.'

'For Maria Esperanza?'

'That's right,' Spendlove said and he managed a small smile over chasing after a runaway wife, as if he realised the embarrassing position he was in, but was too weak to fight it.

Spendlove said, 'When you talked to her, did she mention me?'

He didn't look at Parker. His eyes were down, gazing at his own hands.

Parker said, 'She didn't say you were married. She only said how she met you at a lecture in Boston, like I told you before.'

'Oh,' Spendlove said.

It was clear that he was disappointed that Maria Esperanza hadn't said more. Parker understood. It was dreadful when you couldn't stop thinking of a woman and you learned that you hardly crossed her mind.

'Somebody else,' Parker said, 'somebody else told me you were in Liberty Street asking for Maria Esperanza's house.'

'Oh,' Spendlove said.

He had a way of getting maximum emotion into small words and it was so sad that Parker had to look away.

'Listen,' Parker said, 'let me buy you a drink. What'll you have, a martini?'

'No, a Cutty straight up, no chaser.'

He didn't sound like a fancy Englishman any more. He hadn't sounded like one for some time now.

They were silent until the drinks came. When they did, Spendlove took a couple of big gulps. Parker could see it was doing him good. Some colour came into his face, not much, but enough to show that he had once been alive.

'That Liberty Street,' Spendlove said, 'what a dump. Compared to what we had in Boston, on Commonwealth Avenue, by Exeter Street, down towards the Harvard Club. Compared to that, it's a dump. Compared to anything, that Liberty Street is a dump.'

He put a lot of emphasis on the name Liberty. It hadn't ever occurred to Parker before that there was anything ironic about the name, he had been born and brought up there and he had never thought of the name in any special way.

'Well,' Spendlove said, 'she was looking for her liberty, and I guess she's found it, and what did it turn out to be, a corpse strangled in the ground-floor rear?'

He smiled. The whisky was leading to cynicism and that made him feel better. Cynicism had a bad name, but, Parker thought, it had its uses. When a man was down, cynicism came in handy.

Spendlove finished his Cutty Sark and ordered another. The waitress this time was Kimberly Naundorff. She didn't acknowledge Spendlove and he didn't give her much of a second look. But she winked at Parker. He thought he understood the wink. It meant that Parker had his murderer.

32

Spendlove had another slug of Cutty and said, 'The trouble is, she was a believer. She kept believing, even when I told her it was a phoney.'

'Believed what?'

'All that hooey.'

Spendlove was feeling better. He was talking again in a voice that might have been mistaken for an Englishman's. Parker reckoned the accent was good for convincing people that he was something like a professor when Spendlove was selling reincarnation.

'I told her it was all a bunch of hooey. When we were married, when we were living together as man and wife, I said, "How can you be a good Catholic girl and believe that stuff?" She said, "There's something there." I said, "Sure there is, suckers with money, that's what's there." '

Spendlove looked over the top of his glass at Parker.

'Do I shock you?' he asked. Before Parker could answer he said, 'I shocked her. I really did. I should have continued lying to her, but I couldn't believe she didn't know it was a phoney, just a part of show business to entertain the bored.'

Parker was shocked. Had anyone asked him if he believed in reincarnation, he would have attempted to make a joke, saying that once was enough for him. But Parker had liked the idea of Spendlove being able to remember having lived past lives. Parker had believed in the brush salesman who'd been caught in the hotel fire in Budapest back in 1894. Had Spendlove said he'd been a bigshot in a past life, Parker wouldn't have believed, but Spendlove reducing himself to a not too successful seller of brushes had made Parker see the salesman, looking a bit seedy in old-time clothes, checking into the hotel with his sample cases and then smelling smoke. Parker supposed it showed how clever Spendlove was, presenting himself in a past life as someone very ordinary.

Parker wondered if Spendlove was being clever about the murders. He looked so much like a crazy killer that no one with any common sense would believe he was one. There might be a bluff in that. For all Parker knew, he might be putting on a performance now in that wrinkled suit and the grin that was like the living dead in an old horror movie.

'Does she still believe?' Parker asked.

'Not in me she doesn't. That's why she left.'

'But she believes in herself?'

'She does. After I admitted I was a phoney, she sat there looking me right in the eye, telling me her powers were real. I had to laugh. She didn't like that. But the horrible thing is – ' Spendlove paused and looked about in case anyone was listening ' . . . The terrible thing is, I love her. I always did. Since the first time I saw her.'

It should have been comic and Parker thought that later on it would be, when he thought about it or told someone like Davy Shea about it, Spendlove's confession would be funny. But right now it wasn't. Parker was embarrassed and had to look away for a moment.

Spendlove said, 'I thought it was going to be all right. When I heard Julia was dead and I knew she had left me provided for, I thought it was going to be all right. But it wasn't. When I went to Maria Esperanza and told her I'd be rich, it didn't make any difference to her. She still didn't want to know. How do you like that?'

Parker left the College Inn feeling that Spendlove had very successfully sidetracked him, getting him interested in a romantic tale of unrequited love and away from the motive for Julia Naundorff's murder.

He thought he'd better go see Maria Esperanza to find out how Mrs H. P. Spendlove felt about it.

33

Estelle Ritter was leaning out of an upstairs window when Parker got to the house on Liberty Street. She said without being asked. 'Maria's in the ground-floor rear now and she's at home.'

Estelle pushed the button that opened the front door and it was working today and Parker went in and knocked at the door of Elroy Green's old room.

He could hear Maria Esperanza inside, but she didn't come to the door. He knocked again and waited, thinking it was pretty cool of the estranged Mrs Spendlove to take up residence in Elroy Green's rooms – unless she was hiding something that Davy Shea and Bob Vanderland had failed to uncover. Parker liked Maria Esperanza, but he knew he shouldn't trust anyone.

He knocked some more and the door opened and Maria Esperanza said, 'I told you I had to have time to think,' and then she saw it was Parker and she said, 'Oh, I thought it was someone else.'

Parker came into the room thinking how it was easy to see why a man like Spendlove, an ugly man who was not young any more, would fall for her. When Spendlove learned that Julia Naundorff was in North Holford, he might see his opportunity and kill her to get the money to buy back Maria Esperanza. But how did he do it if he did? How did he kill Julia Naundorff in broad daylight without anyone seeing? Without even Jack Coolidge, who saw it, seeing how it was done?

She sat down and crossed her legs, looking again like a woman that a man might kill for.

She said, 'So you know about me and Archie? I guess it

doesn't take much of a detective to learn that, not the way Archie's been carrying on.'

'Archie?' Parker said. He was confused. Maria Esperanza might be the sort who'd have several men killing for her.

'Yeah, Archie, that's what I call him. In Spanish you say *archie pay* for H. P. So I called him Archie.'

'Cute,' Parker said.

She didn't get the sarcasm.

'Yeah,' she said, 'I used to think it was kind of cute. That was before he changed.'

Parker thought that if she did have the power, she ought to have been able to see that Spendlove was a pathetic case, a sad man who was dying with love for her. Even Parker, who had never seen an aura, could tell that, but she wasn't behaving like a fortune-teller today. Perhaps she's taking the day off, he told himself.

'Yes,' she said, 'I used to think Archie was really something, but not any more.'

'This is a murder investigation,' Parker said to make sure she knew he was being serious.

Then she said, 'I see what you mean. You think Archie might have done it.'

'Him or someone else.'

'You mean me?'

'Why not?'

'Say,' she said, 'I don't know if I like that. You come busting in here and accuse me of murder. Who am I supposed to have killed?'

'You had an opportunity to kill Elroy Green.'

'Yeah,' she said, 'I suppose I did.'

She wasn't angry any more. She was amused. She looked at Parker with a smile on her dark and sexy Latin face.

'Archie's stalking me,' she said. 'He's been out there in the street every night, walking back and forth. I've stood watching him, that's why I'm such a wreck today. I was up all night at the window watching him. It's been like that for a week. If anyone gets himself killed one of these nights, I've got an alibi for Archie. Of course he did have a motive for killing that actress. He was going to get her money. He thought he could buy me with it. When he heard that movie star was dead he said, "We're going to be all right now, Maria." I said, "There's not going to be any all right about you and me ever again, Archie." That took him by surprise. He thought the money would make a difference. He didn't realise I didn't care about money. I had believed in him. I really did. Then I learned he was a phoney. He told me so himself, like fooling all those people was something he was proud of. Well, that was what he knew. He was mistaken about that.'

Parker said, 'Don't you know about the money?'

'What about it?'

'There isn't any. At least not millions or even one million.'

'No kidding?'

Parker thought she was going to laugh. From the way she'd been and what she'd said about Spendlove, he thought she might burst out laughing at the idea of there being no money from Julia Naundorff. He thought she'd be like Kimberly Naundorff and find it wonderfully comic about Spendlove getting let down like that. But she didn't laugh, she didn't even smile.

'Poor Archie,' she said.

After a while she said, 'Do you think he might believe again?'

Parker didn't know what she meant.

She said, 'I'm sure he used to believe. He wouldn't have got to the top of his field without having faith in what he was doing.'

'I don't know,' Parker said. 'He's pretty shattered now. About you – not the money.'

'Now that he's down and out,' she said, 'the belief might come back to him.'

She raised her head, looking at Parker as though she

wanted him to say something reassuring.

'Maybe,' Parker said.

It didn't sound very reassuring to him but she seemed satisfied.

'Yes,' she said, 'That would be nice. If the belief came back, he'd be his old self and not just some crook.'

She looked at Parker to see if he understood. He tried to make a face that might look as if he were giving it very serious consideration, like someone contemplating the conversion of a sinner.

She said, 'I suppose someone like you could never understand.'

'I suppose not,' Parker said. Then he said, 'You know the day Elroy Green was killed, you thought you saw someone in the backyard.'

'Yeah?'

'You said it was someone strange. What'd you mean by that?'

'I don't know. There was something peculiar about him.'

'Nothing about him has come back to you?'

'Not yet. I was hoping being in this room might help.'

'You mean some sort of vibration?'

'Something like that,' she said.

'I was thinking,' Parker said, 'of something more in the line of a simple description, nothing supernatural.'

'The supernatural is all around us,' she said.

'I suppose so,' Parker said.

He sat looking at her bleached blonde hair and he had a sense of dread. It was like a presence of evil. He could see her lying strangled or with her throat cut.

'You've got to watch out,' he said.

'What do you mean?'

She was looking at Parker as though she couldn't understand what he was talking about.

He said, 'I'm worried about you. People know you saw someone in the backyard.'

146

'That's not my destiny,' she said.

'Just the same, be careful.'

He got up to leave. At the door he turned back towards her. He wanted to say something else to give her more of a warning. She stood waiting for him to speak, but he thought he had worried her enough and he said nothing.

'Listen,' she said, 'if there's anything I can do for you. If you want me to remember what I saw in the yard, Archie could do it. He uses hypnosis to get people to reveal their past reincarnations. He could hypnotise me so I'd remember every detail of what I saw in the backyard.'

Parker felt like smiling but he didn't, she was serious.

'That's an idea,' he said.

She came across the room and said, 'If you see Archie, will you tell him I'm sorry about him not getting the big money.'

Parker left. Outside, Estelle Ritter was sitting on the stoop.

'Boomer,' she said, 'is that girl safe?'

'Have you been listening?'

Parker smiled when he said it.

'Of course I've been listening. It's my house. I've already had the notoriety of one dead man. It's because she's a blonde, isn't it? The killer's a crazy person who kills blondes.'

'I don't know,' Parker said.

'You should know,' Estelle said. She got up. She was holding Parker by the arm. 'You're the police now, you should know.'

34

Parker went to the station. Georgie Stover was there.

Parker said. 'Listen, Georgie, you remember the day Davy and I found Elroy Green?'

'I don't think I could forget it.'

Parker said, 'We were heading to Liberty Street and we got a call about a domestic in Hadley Falls. You remember that?'

'Oh, yeah,' Georgie said, 'it was a phoney, wasn't it?'

'That's right.'

'I checked to see where the call came from,' Georgie said, 'it was a public phone. We get a lot of phoney calls.'

'That's true,' Parker said, 'but it kept us from arriving in Liberty Street in time to save Elroy Green.'

Parker tried to remember how many people knew that he and Davy were going to see Elroy Green in the house on Liberty Street. There was Georgie Stover, of course, and Spa Johnson, and there was someone else too. He had forgotten about Ann West.

He'd been at her house getting the list of stolen articles when Davy phoned to say that Spa had remembered Elroy's last name and where he lived.

'I told her,' Parker said to himself, 'I was sitting at the kitchen table looking at her and thinking she was a splendid sight and the call came and I told her.'

He couldn't believe what he was thinking. He had checked Ann's story about having gone out shopping the morning her sister was killed. He'd felt guilty about doing it and he's felt even more guilty when her story checked. He tried to imagine Ann West strangling Elroy Green just as he had tried to imagine Maria Esperanza doing it. Ann was a strong woman, like Maria Esperanza, probably even stronger. She could have done it. But why should she be involved? She couldn't have killed Julia. She had an alibi. Even without that, what motive would she have? She knew that Julia's money wouldn't be coming to her. The farm, of course did, but Ann West already had the farm, she didn't need Julia dead.

'Was there anyone here that day in the station when I was out at Ann West's house?'

'Spa Johnson was here.'

'Yes, yes, I know that. Anyone else?'

'I don't know,' Georgie said. He looked as if he was trying hard to think and it was a big effort.

'Oh yes,' Georgie said, 'that Hollywood guy came in.'

'Which Hollywood guy?'

'The short fat one.'

'Sal Sallas?'

'That's the one,' Georgie said.

35

'Do you know a reason why anyone would want Julia Naundorff dead?' Parker asked Sally Sallas.

He had driven straight to the Lake House Hotel to see Sallas.

'You bet I do,' Sallas said.

It wasn't the answer Parker expected. Asking a question like that, he thought Sallas would be evasive.

They were sitting in the bar at the Lake House. It was past dinner time but there were still people in the dining-room. Parker could see the manageress standing just inside the dining-room door keeping an eye on the customers. Parker knew her. She was a good-looking woman wearing a lot of make-up. Sallas saw her too.

'She's a looker,' he said, 'but past her prime. That type peaks early, sometimes about her last year in high school. Often a girl like that gets her head full of ideas, people paying her compliments and high school guys going nuts for her. She thinks she'll make it in the movies, but her looks don't last – only she don't know it and there's a tragedy with her hanging round LA going to hell real fast.'

He spoke with the detached earnestness of a professional.

'Julia Naundorff,' Parker said, 'you say people wanted to see her dead.'

'It's a fact. They did.'

'Why was that? Why would they want her dead?'

He could see Sallas's eyes move back to the entrance to the dining-room. He thought the manageress must be moving about. She might have peaked early, but she was still good to watch when she was in motion.

'Why?' Sallas said. His eyes came back to Parker. 'Because she was a bitch. A first-class bitch, that's why.'

He seemed happy being able to tell Parker this.

'How was she a bitch?' Parker asked.

'You mean how did it manifest itself? At work, and in her private life. Mostly in the way she treated guys. Real bad, that's how she treated them, and women she simply ignored.'

Parker wondered if Coolidge was one of those she had treated bad. He had seen Coolidge in the magazine photo looking not particularly happy at Sally's Oscar night party. He had been standing alongside Julia in that expensive dress and Julia had looked very happy, but Coolidge looked like a man who had only come to escort the garment. Not that one single photo told you much. It could have been only a trick of light, catching Coolidge between smiles.

'Was Jack Coolidge one of those men?' Parker asked.

'He might have been, but he wasn't. He was too smart. He knew his place, which was being a mere writer in a town where writers don't count for much. He knew she was a hundred percent bitch. He took care of himself. But I see what you mean. You're wondering if Jack could have killed her, with me in on it too, naturally.'

'I don't wish to be impolite,' Parker said, 'but it crossed my mind.'

Sallas smiled.

'That's good,' he said. 'I don't wish to be impolite, but are you a murderer? I like that. The reluctant detective. But you've got to understand about Jack. He's not a real Hollywood guy. He's not even Los Angeles. He's a regular backwoods Jack London. He's in his element here. He couldn't be happier than never changing his shirt, going out fishing before the worms are even up. I said to Jack, "Jack, we ought to get out of here." But he wouldn't budge. "Sally," he said, "I want to find out what happens." That's the writer in him, he wants to find out how the story is going to end. I said to him, "I'll tell you what's going to happen, the cops here are going to start looking for a couple of out-of-towners to pin it on." I was right, wasn't I? You're all set to pin it on us now?'

'It'd be handy.'

'I like that. "It'd be handy." I'll bet it would. But a couple of guys who wanted to zero a woman wouldn't come out in broad daylight in their brand new plaid shirts and new store-bought fishing poles to do it. They'd sneak around so no one could see.'

'Do you know men who would have liked to sneak around and done it?' Parker asked.

'Like I said, plenty – and nobody who'd blame them.'

'You don't mean guys in the Mob?'

'You like that idea, don't you? That'd make it plenty easy for you if it was the Mob. Nobody would expect you to catch anyone if it was the Mob.'

That was true but Parker didn't say so. Sallas said: 'She hung around with some of the boys. A couple of them in particular. But she was smart enough to know she shouldn't try to give them the finger. If she ever owed them money she paid it back. I know that for a fact. Otherwise she was free and easy with money, she thought success would last for ever. I told her it wouldn't, but she didn't believe me. So she died broke. Or at least what she'd call broke.'

Parker had heard this before from Coolidge, and he thought there must be a bored expression on his face that showed, because Sallas smiled like an entertainer who knew that he's losing his audience but still has a couple of good stories up his sleeve.

He said, 'To show you what a bitch she was, I'll tell you something which not a lot of people know.'

He looked around as if suspecting that someone might be spying on him. Then he said in a confidential voice, 'When she married Brad Donzil, who was getting to be a biggie and was going to get bigger, she said, "It'll be good for my career, Sal. I hope you don't mind." I said, "Why should I mind?" She looked at me, one of those looks like I was a kid hiding something in his pocket and she says, "Because I've got the hots for you, Sal, and I always thought maybe you had the hots for me." It was amazing. I had never had the hots for her, but when she said it I started to have them real bad. It was incredible. I spent a week with her in Mexico the week before she married Brad. I felt a louse. Brad was on my books too. At the wedding I didn't know where to look. When I finally got the nerve to look at her, she smiled at me like I was a distant cousin from some place like Canada. Boy, that shook me, the nerve she had. Of course I'm only a short fat guy, I never got much practice being a swordsman, not without paying good money upfront.'

'Brad Donzil?' Parker said.

'Where you been you don't know Brad?' Sallas said. 'He never killed nobody. He died. He was always exercising. He had a heart attack and died. You've got a guy in town who's crazy enough,' he said, 'that reincarnation guy,

Spendlove. I can see him killing Julia. The money she's going to leave may be peanuts to big-time people, but it won't be peanuts to him.'

Parker said, 'You dropped in the station the day Julia Naundorff was found dead. Why'd you do that?'

'I wanted to leave town. Jack didn't, but I did. I came to the station to find out if it was all right to leave, but you weren't there. Later on Jack talked me into staying.'

His eyes moved off Parker. Parker thought the good-looking manageress must be moving about again in the entrance to the dining-room, but Sallas said, 'There's the sister. Julia's sister. She's got class. A certain kind of style. You won't catch her peaking and then losing it on account of she's never been flashy. Understated, that's what it is, and it lasts longer than flash.'

Parker turned around to look at Ann.

Sallas said, 'See, understated, no make-up. Not on her mouth, not on her eyes. What she's got, it's going to last for ever.'

Ann's golden blonde head was coming out of the dining-room. She was walking towards the front door. Whitey Gotton was with her.

'That guy with her,' Sallas said, 'I know him. He used to be a big-league pitcher, he was a guy who knew what kind of a bitch Julia Naundorff was.'

36

In the morning Parker went to Old Compton to see Whitey Gotton.

When he walked into the store Whitey was behind the counter serving an old man, but he saw Parker come in and he said, 'I'll be right with you, Boomer.'

Then he went back to serving the old man.

Parker stood around and waited, looking at the masses of fishing tackle Whitey had on display, and at the photos and framed newspaper pages on the wall.

There was a pale space on the wall where one of the pictures had been taken down.

Parker went over and looked at the blank space. It was where the picture of Whitey autographing a baseball for Julia Naundorff had been.

Parker turned and saw Whitey was looking at him. Whitey smiled. It was one of those quick nervous smiles that a kid might use when he was caught out doing something. Whitey was like a kid, Parker thought, he'd spent his entire life playing a boy's game and when he was forced out of the game, he took up another game. Parker thought that Whitey probably didn't have much experience with grown-up emotion. Maybe when a woman annoyed him, did him wrong the way a Hollywood actress like Julia Naundorff was supposed to have done men wrong, Whitey might react in a violent way, like a kid would do.

Whitey finished with the old man. He didn't make a sale. The old man left the shop with the slow walk of a man who has got nothing really to do and so thinks he'd best make the most out of simply walking across a floor.

'How'd you like that?' Whitey said. 'He said he had to think over buying a lousy thirty-nine-buck lure. I should have told him not to take too much time because he ain't got all that much time left. That's what I should have said.'

Parker wondered what Ann West saw in Whitey. 'Maybe she's a baseball fan,' he said to himself. 'And he's helping his sister with her three daughters. A woman might like that. See a noble side to a man who was doing that.'

'Well,' Whitey said, 'what can I do for you? Are you going to take up fishing, or is this some more cop stuff?'

'Cop stuff,' Parker said. 'The other day you told me you didn't know Julia Naundorff.'

'Did I say that? I don't remember.'

'Are you changing your story?'

'What story is that?'

'About her.'

'Do I have a story about her?'

'I understand you do.'

'Who told you that, that fat Hollywood guy?'

Parker didn't say anything.

Whitey said, 'I guessed he might tell you something like that.'

'Would he have to make it up?'

'You tell me,' Whitey said.

'Tell you what?' Parker said.

'Tell me if balling a woman a couple three times is a *story*. For some guys, I suppose, that is something to write home about, for others it isn't. Know what I mean?'

Parker reckoned he did.

'That was it?' he said.

'I guess so,' Whitey said, 'and it was a long time ago, and I wasn't the Lone Ranger. I'm not even the only guy in town who just happens to have had a time with her. Ask the fat guy. He was balling her too. Can you imagine that? It makes you think. A guy might think he was something, balling a movie star, but then he looks around and sees who else is also getting into her pants, he has to think again. Also that other guy, the fat man's friend. And maybe the crazy reincarnation guy. Who knows? And why not, the way she was?'

'You seem to know a lot about it.'

'I've got a source of information.'

Parker supposed he did, but he couldn't see Ann West telling it the same way Whitey did.

Parker decided to leave, but he looked again at the blank space on the wall.

'You took her picture down,' he said. 'Why'd you do that?'

'Respect,' Whitey said. 'You got to have some respect for the dead.'

37

When he left Whitey, Parker decided he'd go to the Lakeside Players and see what had happened to Spa Johnson's theatrical career.

Even early in the morning the amusement park was noisy and crowded. The rollercoaster was full of people screaming. Parker drove directly to the theatre.

When he asked for Dick Doyle the woman at the box office smiled.

'I wouldn't know where he is,' she said. 'At least I've got an idea where he is, but I'm not saying. You better ask Lillian. She's backstage.'

No one was guarding the stage door and Parker walked right in. Someone was screaming at someone else and he thought it must be the play they were rehearsing for next week.

The screaming stopped and a young woman came running to where Parker was standing. She was in tears.

'She's a bitch,' she said to Parker, 'a real goddam bitch.'

She looked like she wanted to run away, but didn't know where to run to. There was the sound of laughter from the stage and then the tramp of heavy feet.

'She's going to kill me,' the young woman said.

The heavy footsteps got closer and then Lillian Hauser arrived. She didn't seem big enough to be making that much noise with her feet.

The frightened actress put Parker between herself and Lillian Hauser, who was so angry that she didn't seem to see Parker.

'Clare, you little whore,' Lillian said, 'tell me where he is.'

'I don't know,' Clare said.

'Sure you do,' Lillian said, 'everyone knows but me.'

She noticed Parker.

'You,' she said, 'what are you doing here?'

'Looking for Dick.'

It didn't seem the right thing to say.

'That bastard,' Lillian said. 'I'm looking for him too. And when I catch him you're going to have another murder on your hands. Don't laugh. It isn't funny.'

'I'm not laughing,' Parker said.

'I'm not talking to you,' Lillian said.

'I didn't laugh,' Clare said.

'You smiled.'

'It was a nervous reaction.'

'Jesus, what a klutz,' Lillian said.

She seemed more amused now than angry.

'Get out of my sight,' she said to the girl. 'And if you can't remember where that bastard Doyle is, at least try to remember some of your lines.'

Clare went back to the stage, moving wide round Lillian in case she might strike her.

'What do you expect?' Lillian said when Clare had gone. 'Of course I can't pay them much and what they all want is to be in the movies, they don't care about the theatre.'

Then she looked at Parker as though realising she was wasting her time talking to him.

'What are you doing here?' she asked.

'Still looking for Doyle.'

'You better join the line.'

She glanced about as though she might see Doyle hiding somewhere.

'What do you want to see him for?' she asked. 'Of course you think he might have killed Julia. I don't suppose I should tell you this, but I was worried when Julia Naundorff came here. I thought she might have it in her mind to start up with Doyle again.' She glanced at Parker to make sure he was taking in what she was saying. 'They had a thing,' she said. 'Did you know that?'

Parker said he didn't know.

'Jesus,' Lillian said, 'I really shouldn't be telling you this. You must think I'm the most awful crazy bitch, but when she was found dead, the first thing I thought of was Dick.'

It took Parker some time to realise what she was saying, but then what she said next dispelled any doubt he might have had.

'The morning she was killed he wasn't with me. He hadn't been home and I knew he'd seen her that night.'

Lillian looked at Parker again to make sure he got it. She was so tiny compared to Parker that she had to look far up and she tilted her head to the side as she did it as if she didn't want to hurt her neck.

'There,' she said, 'I did it. I didn't want to. I wasn't going to say anything. But now I think, why should I protect him? And the woman is dead. Somebody killed her.'

Parker didn't know what to say. It didn't seem right to thank her.

'Are you sure he saw Julia Naundorff the night before?'

'Of course I'm sure. I saw them.'

She was annoyed at Parker doubting her word. She said, 'Do you think I like telling you this?'

It was actually what Parker was thinking.

'I followed him,' she said. 'I feel ashamed admitting it, but that's what I did. Have you any idea how awful that makes you feel? I suppose you don't. You're a cop, you're used to shadowing people.'

'Did Dick spend the night with her?'

Lillian became agitated. She gave her head a little shake, as though trying to get rid of an unpleasant memory. 'I suppose he did. I didn't see. I saw him meet her and I saw them go off together. If he didn't spend the night with her, why didn't he come home? But then of course he's a drunken Irish bum, sometimes he gets so damned drunk he can't find his way home. People call to tell me he's out cold on their sofas, but sometimes they don't call.'

She was the long-suffering woman now, not the woman who had just accused her man of murder.

'Where did he meet her that night?' Parker asked.

'In a bar. In Lobo's Rathskeller Bar and Grill. I saw him go in and I waited and saw them come out. I was around the corner waiting. They didn't see me in the dark.'

'Are you sure it was Julia Naundorff?'

'Of course it was her. I couldn't mistake that blonde head of hair, and the way she walked.'

'And they seemed to be getting on?'

'What do you mean? Of course they were getting on. They were together.'

'And in the morning he killed her? That seems a big leap.'

'Maybe you don't understand men and women. A lot of things can happen in one night. He was crazy about her. I told you that. He pretended it was over, but I could tell.'

'Had he been in touch with her?'

'I don't know. He wouldn't have told me. I'd be the last person he'd tell. But he never talked about her. He never mentioned her.'

She looked at Parker as though trying to assess how clever he was, if he was intelligent enough to grasp what she was saying.

'Ordinarily,' she said, 'in our business, there's always gossip or funny stories people tell, especially about someone they used to know who's made it big. You'd think Dick would have told stories about Julia Naundorff, but he never did.'

It didn't seem like solid evidence to Parker, but he supposed Lillian Hauser knew her man.

Something else bothered him. When Julia Naundorff came to North Holford, the whole township had been interested and then disappointed because she never appeared in town. If she'd gone to even a dark and dingy place like Lobo's, somebody would have noticed.

159

'Of course,' he said, 'you've just told me that you had a good motive for killing her.'

Parker was walking to his car when he heard running feet behind him and he turned to see Clare, the young actress Lillian had been shouting at.

'You're looking for Dick?' she said. 'I know where he is, but don't tell Ma Hauser I know.'

Parker said he'd keep her out of it.

'He's at the Pine Rest. Do you know it?'

Parker did. It was a motel out on the old highway at Hadley Falls.

'He's a good guy,' Clare said. 'He ought to know what that old bitch is saying about him, accusing him of murder.'

She had also involved herself, but he didn't say anything.

38

The route to the Pine Rest took Parker by Lobo's Rathskeller and he stopped and went in, but no one could remember seeing Dick Doyle or Julia Naundorff in there that night. Lobo's was a place that had trouble remembering things.

Parker couldn't see Dick Doyle taking a woman like Julia Naundorff into a run-down bar like Lobo's, but then maybe it was a perfect place to take her. No one would expect to see a movie star there.

Lobo's was a criminal hangout. There were drug dealers in one corner and they hardly stopped dealing when Parker came in. In another part of the bar there were a bunch of under-age drinkers. They all knew that Parker was a cop, but it didn't bother them. Lobo's was one of the places the mayor wanted cracked down on. Lobo had been paying off the old police chief and Parker had been brought in to stop that.

'Julia Naundorff in here?' Lobo said. 'The movie actress? Are you kidding?'

Several heads turned to see if Parker was kidding. When they saw he wasn't, they smiled. Parker's reputation for being goofy would be growing.

Parker went out and drove the old DeSoto out to Hadley Falls, past the house where the old couple lived that he and Davy had been called to on the day Elroy Green was killed.

Parker thought he might have trouble finding Doyle, at least registered under his own name, but when he pulled into the forecourt of the Pine Rest, the man himself was sitting at a picnic table under the shade of some pine trees, looking as if nothing in the world was troubling him. But then, Parker knew he was a good-natured Irishman who seemed to shrug off trouble. It was an ability he needed to possess to live with Lillian Hauser and sometimes not come home at night.

'Boomer,' Doyle said, 'what are you doing here on your own? Are you meeting someone? If so, I haven't seen a thing.'

'I'm meeting you,' Parker said.

'It's not about that Spa Johnson kid is it? I don't know how much of a position I'm in to give him a job. Even only a job with a broom.'

'I heard you were having trouble.'

'And how,' Doyle said. 'Sit down and have a beer.'

Parker sat down but he said he didn't want a beer.

'Is it that serious?' Doyle said.

He was joking, but when he saw Parker's face he stopped smiling.

'What the Christ is it, Boomer?' he asked.

Parker told him what Lillian Hauser had said about Julia Naundorff.

'I've been to Lobo's,' Parker said, 'they don't remember you being there.'

'I was there,' Doyle said. The smile came back to his Irish eyes. They were a deep dark blue that stood out under the black hair.

'You were there with Julia Naundorff?'

'No, not with Julia.' Doyle was amused again. He said, 'Can you imagine Lillian making a mistake like that?'

'She was pretty certain it was Julia Naundorff.'

'She had Julia on the brain. Ever since we heard she had come to stay with Ann West, Lillian hasn't been able to think of anything else. She's been driving me nuts with it.'

'She says you're the one who had Julia Naundorff on the brain.'

'I did,' Doyle said, 'a time long ago. It was quite a shock learning she had come here. She was the last person I wanted to see.' The Irish eyes stopped smiling. 'Jesus Christ, Boomer, you're not getting me involved in this thing, are you?'

'It seems like you are already involved.'

'That was in the past. We were close then, but not now, not any more.'

'How close is close?' Parker asked.

'Oh, Jesus,' Doyle said, 'you're going to find out anyway. We were very close. We lived together. We were going to get married. She was pregnant.'

'Was there a child?'

'No, no,' Doyle said.

He was angry and impatient. Parker could imagine him becoming violent if aroused.

'Something happened?' Parker said.

'You bet it did. She had an abortion.'

It was hard to see Doyle as a family man, but Parker could see him perhaps being troubled by that, he was, after all, an Irish Catholic.

Doyle said, 'It was asking for it getting involved in a

162

serious way with a woman like Julia, but she was so beautiful.'

Parker wondered what Doyle thought he was getting into, becoming involved with a woman like Lillian Hauser, but he didn't say anything, he simply sat there at the picnic table under the pine trees and watched Doyle being shattered. If Doyle were a better actor, Parker thought, he wouldn't let himself be seen like this. He must know the way he's telling the story is grounds for murder, even after all these years. Maybe the years made it worse suddenly seeing Julia Naundorff and looking back at what might have been.

'Who was the woman at Lobo's if it wasn't Julia Naundorff?' Parker asked.

'Clare Egan,' Doyle said.

'The young actress at the theatre? She's got dark hair.'

'She was wearing a wig. She was having a joke.' The way Doyle said it, it was nothing to smile about. 'She didn't know about Julia and me. Not the real story. She got dressed up as Julia because she thought it would give me a laugh, which it didn't.'

'That was that night. What about the morning? Where were you then?'

'You mean when Julia died?'

'When she was murdered.'

'You're serious, aren't you, Boomer? Jesus, this is going to be a terrible undoing. Lillian is going to have a fit.'

'I've got to know.'

'I was here with Clare Egan.'

'In the morning?'

'At night and in the morning.'

'Did anyone see you?'

'They must have.'

'I better talk to Clare Egan,' Parker said.

Doyle looked at his wristwatch. 'I'll call her. She'll be free now.' He called her and asked her to come to the Pine Rest.

He said, 'So she accused me of murder, did she? The bitch. Well, she can't have any complaints about my behaviour after this. If a lad goes out and gets drunk, she won't be able to say a thing.'

He smiled at the prospect ahead.

'This calls for a drink,' he said. 'This is a good place, very nice and peaceful, a man can have a good bash here.'

He got himself a drink and then he got some more and he was in a good mood when Clare Egan came in all out of breath as if she had run from the theatre instead of taking a car.

'What's going on, Dick?' she said. 'I had to duck away from Lillian. Even so she's suspicious. I brought the blonde wig like you said.'

She put it on. She didn't look anything like Julia Naundorff.

'Fix it right,' Doyle said, 'don't just clamp it on your head like a tea cozy.'

'A tea what?' Clare asked.

'Never mind,' Dick said.

The girl arranged the wig.

'There,' Doyle said, 'there's the Julia Naundorff that Lillian bloody Hauser saw coming out of Lobo's Rathskeller.'

It did seem very convincing to Parker.

'Do the walk,' Doyle said to the girl.

'I feel silly,' Clare said. 'In the daylight like this.'

'Christ, you're supposed to be an actress,' Doyle said.

Clare turned and walked away from them.

'That's Julia's walk,' Doyle said.

Parker supposed that in the dark it would be convincing, especially to a woman who wanted to see Doyle stepping out with Julia Naundorff.

'What are you going to do now, Boomer?' Doyle asked. 'Do you have any more friends you can try to pin it on?'

'Leave him alone,' Clare said, 'he's only a cop.'

'I need a drink,' Doyle said. 'I need several big drinks.'

164

He was sitting on the bench at the table, under the trees. Clare sat down beside him and held his hands.

'Do you really think you should?' she said.

'You bet,' Doyle said. 'You bet I do.'

39

In the station Parker asked Davy, 'What do you know about Whitey Gotton and Julia Naundorff? I found out he knew her in Los Angeles.'

'Everyone knew that,' Davy said.

'I didn't know it,' Parker said.

'Well,' Davy said, 'there are a lot of things you don't seem to know that everyone else knows, like never having seen Julia Naundorff in a picture. Everyone knew Whitey was dating the movie star. They knew about him and Naundorff, it was in the *Holford Transcript*, with pictures.'

'When was that?'

'Oh, I don't know. A long time ago, when Whitey was still playing ball.'

'You didn't think that was something worth telling me?'

'Whitey was somewhere else when she was killed.'

'So was everybody,' Parker said.

'Not entirely, there's been a new development. I think we've got our man.'

Davy glanced across the room. There was a young woman sitting by the big open window. Her head was turned and he couldn't see her face. There was a child sitting on her lap. The breeze from the window blew the woman's hair and the child tried to grab it.

The woman turned her head and Parker recognised Louise Leclerc. The black eye had faded, but she had a new bruise on her face. She looked pathetic with her battered face. Holding the child, it was like *Madonna and Child* in a hick police station, instead of a stable.

'Look at this,' Davy said.

He had an expensive leather suitcase on his desk. He opened it and there was the rich gleam of antique silver.

'See the initials,' Davy said. The initials J. N. were on the suitcase. 'Julia Naundorff,' Davy said.

Louise stood up, clutching the child.

'I didn't want to tell on Dean,' she said, 'but with my own sister, that really got to me.'

'That's the way it is,' Davy said to Parker. 'You go around looking for fancy clues and trying to figure out motive and opportunity and then some woman walks in and squeals on the guy.'

'You sure it's Julia Naundorff's suitcase?' Parker said.

'I'm sure. Besides, your friend Ann West is coming down to identify it.'

'When was it stolen?'

'The day of the murders,' Davy said. 'Dean Judd came back home with it.'

Parker was embarrassed. He'd screwed up. He hadn't checked Dean Judd's alibi about being in Holford on the morning of Julia's death looking for a job as a busdriver.

'I never really looked at the suitcase,' Louise said.

'I'll bet you didn't,' Davy said. 'You hold back evidence when there was a murder investigation going on, and only come forward when you caught him playing games with your sister. You're in deep trouble.'

Parker looked at Louise and thought that trouble had been with her all her life. He didn't think Davy's threat scared her. She sat down again and looked at Parker.

'What about that?' she asked. 'Can he get away with charging me?'

'I don't think so,' Parker said. She'd worn the Versace dress that Elroy Green had given her without realising where it came from. She might not have taken much notice of a classy suitcase. It would have been just another example of the glamorous objects that sometimes came into her view, having no more reality than something seen on TV. Besides, they were going to need her to give evidence. Davy would have to ease up on Louise Leclerc if they wanted her as a witness.

'It'll be all right,' Parker said to her.

'Will it?' Davy said.

'Yes,' Parker said, 'I don't want her treated like a criminal. She came in on her own and volunteered the information. We can't lock her up.'

'Anything you say, Boomer,' Davy said, 'you say I should let her go, I'll let her go.'

Davy smiled. He was so pleased by his sarcasm that he wasn't angry any more.

The door opened and Ann West came in, looking like she had just stepped off a tractor. She was wearing a dirty T-shirt, old jeans and a pair of brown boots with big heavy soles.

Ann gave Parker a big smile as if they were old friends.

Parker managed to take his eyes off Ann and saw the way Louise was looking at her. In spite of the old jeans and the dirty T-shirt, Parker could see that Louise saw her as a rich woman, something beyond her, like the stolen suitcase.

Davy said, 'Is this your sister's case, Miss West?'

'I guess so,' Ann said, 'it's flashy enough.'

'And these?' Davy said.

He opened the case and there was the splendid gleam of old silver.

'Goodness,' Ann said.

She was surprised and amused.

'That's expensive stuff,' Davy said, 'worth a lot of money.'

'It is,' Ann said. 'It's Georgian.'

'It was your sister's?' Davy asked.

'I knew she had a collection of silver. She told me, but

I've never seen it. She came with so much stuff. She had so many suitcases.'

Davy said, 'These are fine pieces. Wonderful things. Look at those hallmarks. Really old, fine stuff.'

Parker looked at Louise. She had recognised the silver as something rich that Dean Judd could only have got by stealing, but she took no interest in it now. She held her face up, letting the breeze from the window blow her hair. The child was asleep. Catching Judd with her kid sister was a shattering thing, Parker thought, betrayal made her seek revenge. Still, he saw that before she came to tell on him she had stopped to put make-up on.

Ann said, 'Can I go now? I've got a horse that's poorly. I've got to pack his hoof with Stockholm tar. I was in the middle of doing that when I was called here.'

'I guess that'll be all right,' Davy said.

Parker watched Ann cross to the door. Then he saw that Davy was looking at him and he turned away.

Louise, holding the child, still stood by the window with the breeze blowing through her hair.

'There she is now,' she said, looking out of the window, 'there's the little whore.'

The door of the station opened. Georgie Stover came in with Suzanne Leclerc. Behind him Dean Judd was being held by a regular cop called Ed Ross and by the summer cop Bob Vanderland. Judd wasn't struggling, but he had been hit. One eye was swollen and he had a cut lip.

'How do you like your boyfriend now?' Louise said to her sister.

Suzanne wasn't listening to her. She was frightened.

'I didn't have nothing to do with murders,' she said to Parker. 'If there were any murders it was all him.'

'Listen to her,' Louise said. 'That's some girlfriend.'

'What about you?' her sister said. 'Calling in the cops?'

'I'm not his girlfriend any more,' Louise said, 'I've become a good citizen instead.'

168

'Whore,' Suzanne said.

'Me?' Louise said. 'You're the whore.'

'Never mind the domestic,' Davy said to them, 'we've got all the domestics we want, we don't have to send out for any new ones.'

He pushed Judd towards the desk with the silver.

'Listen,' Parker said, 'how'd he get that eye and that lip? Did you give it to him, Bob?'

Parker had had to speak to Vanderland several times about roughing up drunks and kids who got out of hand at beach parties.

'He got lippy,' Vanderland said. 'I thought he was going to run.'

Suzanne turned to her sister. 'Louise,' she said, 'what the hell have you done, bringing the cops down on us?'

'Listen,' Louise said, 'we're better off away from the guy.'

She had her hand on Suzanne's arm. Suzanne bowed her head. 'Yeah,' she said, 'I know.' She seemed about to cry.

'It'll be all right,' Louise told her. 'Later on you'll meet someone nice.'

Suzanne's head was still bowed. 'Yeah,' she said.

Parker glanced at Dean Judd to see how he was taking this betrayal. He didn't seem to be taking any notice. He was a tough kid and although he might know about car engines, he didn't look too bright.

'You got anything to say for yourself?' Parker asked him.

'Look,' Judd said, 'I went into the house to see if there was anything worth stealing, but somebody had got there already. I saw a lot of suitcases in the bedroom and I picked up this one and it was heavy and I opened it and I saw the silver and so I took it.'

'You didn't meet Billy Zoots and Elroy Green there?' Davy said. 'You didn't kill Billy Zoots in the bushes and Julia Naundorff saw you and so you had to kill her, and then you went to Elroy Green's place in Liberty Street and killed him in case he'd seen something too?'

'I didn't do nothing like that,' Judd said.

'How'd you kill Julia Naundorff?' Parker asked. 'How'd you manage that?'

'I didn't kill no one,' Judd said.

'We'll get it out of him,' Davy said.

'Sure,' Vanderland said.

'We're going to have to lock you up,' Parker said to Judd.

'What the hell's this, Boomer?' Davy said. 'What the hell are you apologising to him for? He done it. He admits he was there. He done it.'

'I wish I could be as sure of that as you are,' Parker said.

'What aren't you sure of, Boomer? He stole the silver, didn't he?'

Judd showed no emotion. Of course not, Parker thought, he's got a lifetime's experience of being on the wrong side of the law. He doesn't expect anything else, and a good thing too, because he's not going to get it if Davy has his way.

Suzanne was a good-looking girl, prettier than her sister, but there was something sly about her, Parker thought, as though she knew things that she thought other people would like to know, but lacked her cleverness and would never know. It was her small eyes in her narrow face that mostly made her appear sly.

She was standing by the open window beside her sister and her hair was also blowing in the breeze. Her hair was long and curled at the ends. She twisted the ends of it around with her fingers as she stood there looking at Judd.

Dean Judd wasn't saying anything. He had been standing with his head bowed, but Parker saw him lift his head now and look at Suzanne.

And then Parker saw that Judd wasn't looking at Suzanne. He was looking at the open window.

'Watch out,' Parker shouted.

Davy stopped talking. He turned to Parker.

'What?' he said.

170

Judd leaped through the window, knocking Louise and the child to one side.

'Jesus,' she said, keeping a quick hold of the child.

Vanderland had his gun out.

'Not in the street,' Parker said, 'don't go shooting in the street.'

Vanderland was leaning out of the window.

'I got a clear shot at him, Boomer,' he said.

Davy said, 'Go for it, shoot the bastard now.'

Vanderland, hanging out of the window, started shooting.

'Oh Jesus!' Suzanne said, 'oh Jesus Christ!'

Vanderland came in from the window.

'He got away,' he said.

Still, he looked pleased about being able to fire his gun in broad daylight down the township's main street.

Ed Ross and Georgie Stover were already out of the door. Parker saw them running down the street with their guns drawn.

'I guess that proves that,' Davy said. 'I guess we don't need any more evidence than Dean Judd pleading guilty with his feet.'

40

Dean Judd left no real trail although there were many reports of sightings, all delivered with an enthusiasm that made up for their vagueness.

Parker sat in his kitchen drinking coffee and waiting for the telephone to ring telling him Judd had been captured.

He thought he should call Julia Naundorff's lawyer and arrange to see her papers. He should have done that as soon as she was found dead. He wasn't a real cop, but he was a real lawyer and he should have acted like one and gone after the papers right away.

He glanced at the clock. It was the wrong time of day to call California. He phoned the College Inn and asked for Kimberly Naundorff.

She had been working late and was probably still asleep, he was told. He had them wake her and she wasn't pleased.

'Listen, Mr Daniels,' Kimberly said, 'I was asleep and dreaming and for once it wasn't about poor Julia, and then you woke me.'

'I'm sorry,' Parker said. Her daughter had died and no one had felt sorry for Kimberly. She had been merely an inconvenience. And Billy Zoots, Parker thought, and Elroy Green, they were also dead and no one had thought about them having mothers whose dreams might be full of them.

'I'll call back later,' he said.

'No, no, I'm up now,' Kimberly said.

Parker told her he wanted to see Julia's papers.

'I don't have them,' she said. 'Ann has them. The lawyer in California sent copies of them to Ann and I think to Sal Sallas too.'

Then she asked how the investigation was going and Parker had to tell her that Dean Judd was on the run.

'Is it true,' she said, 'that you're going to get Spendlove to hypnotise that Puerto Rican woman so she'll remember who she saw in the backyard?'

Parker wondered where she'd got that story and then she told him.

'Spendlove,' she said, 'I see him in the College Inn, he's been bragging about it.'

Parker knew Spendlove would do that, but it was dangerous. It might give the murderer ideas – and Maria Esperanza had yellow hair. That was, of course, if Dean Judd was innocent and the killer was still at large.

Kimberly was saying, 'Old Spendlove, he's crazy. I wanted to hate him, but he's too loony to hate. Besides, he makes me laugh.'

'That's good,' Parker said.

'You bet it is,' she said, 'I'm glad you've got your killer and it isn't Spendlove.'

Parker didn't say anything about that.

41

Parker drove out to Old Compton. It was still early. There was a mist over the lake, it crept in and hung over the fields and drifted between the trees.

Once the mist lifted it would be a hot day. Then the lake would be full of people and boats making noise. But right now it was still. There were fishermen standing on the shore casting their lines, and out on the water he saw several small rowing boats with figures in them making casting motions and a line he couldn't see hitting the water and sending out a ripple. The lake was beautiful, Parker thought, but he couldn't see why a woman like Julia Naundorff, a movie star, would want to live on a farm.

The road ran close to the shore. He saw a woman alone in a rowboat. She wore a red hat. He recognised that beret, and also the shape of the woman as she stood up to make a cast. It was Phyllis Skypeck. She looked very self-contained out on the lake early in the morning all by herself like that, very different from the woman people said was too promiscuous for her own good, or at least for a doctor's own good.

Parker drove on and turned into the rutted drive to Ann's house. He parked the old DeSoto under a big chestnut tree and stood for a moment, looking at the lake where the mist was shining now with the sun about to break through. It had been like this on the morning when he and Davy had come with the Wilson kid to find Billy Zoots lying in the bushes with his amazing yellow hair and his even more amazing cut throat. Billy Zoots had his knife out, but he hadn't had time to use it. Whoever killed him had been too fast for Billy Zoots.

Dean Judd would be quick like that, Parker thought. He'd certainly been quick when he leaped like a wild creature out of the window at the station. Parker couldn't see Sally Sallas being quick, nor Jack Coolidge. One was short and fat and the other was tall and moved in a lazy way like a man who did his work sitting down and only got up to stretch and make himself another cup of coffee.

Someone had had to be quick, too, to get behind Elroy Green in his own room and loop a cord round his neck and strangle him. Then rather than flee the scene, the killer had tied the elaborate fancy knot. Why was that? Was it some sort of joke, a way of teasing the police? It seemed a crazy thing to do. Parker wondered again if they were up against a crazy man who killed people with yellow hair.

He took out his mobile phone and called the station. Dean Judd was still on the loose. Georgie Stover said he thought Judd was probably clear out of the area by now.

Parker stood looking at the lake, thinking that things were not as they seemed. The haze on the water was a curtain, shrouding the scene in secrecy. It was the same with this case, Parker thought, a haze masking the murder of Julia Naundorff. The haze over the water was deceptive itself, making him think of a winter scene even though it was the height of summer.

He turned away and walked towards the house, thinking once again that even if the old farmstead needed paint, it was a splendid place, much better than anything he could ever afford. It was the old feeling, one he had had since he was a kid and a friend from school would invite him into his house and he would feel not jealous, but a complete stranger, afraid to move or to speak in too loud a voice, showing the same sort of respect in a rich house that he might have in a church or temple that belonged to a faith that wasn't his.

Before he reached the kitchen door, Ann came out from the side of a farm building and came towards him with her golden yellow hair swinging, and she was another splendid sight, even in worn cut-down jeans and an old shirt.

'Hello,' she said. She stood looking up at him, with one hand shielding her long grey eyes like she had done that morning when they first met.

He told her why he had come so early this morning.

'Oh dear,' she said, still with her hand up over her eyes, 'I thought you might have come to see me.'

'Well,' Parker said, 'it is a pleasure seeing you.'

He could hear his voice sounding not quite his own.

Ann must have heard it too. She said, 'Don't be gallant, there's no need to lie.'

'It's not a lie,' Parker said. 'Why should it be a lie?'

He felt like a teenage boy who had a thing for a girl who was massively out of his league. Or perhaps he felt like a man who was older than the woman and much too poor.

Parker didn't know what to say. It was enough for him to stand looking at her, but he feared he might be thought rude.

Finally he said, 'You like life in the country?'

'Oh yes, and on a farm in the country. It's what I'm used to.' Then she said, 'I hear you've got your man.'

'Davy Shea has got his man, only he's run away. I'm not so sure.'

'Oh, dear,' she said, 'and I was feeling good about it being settled.'

Parker told her that he'd like to see Julia's papers.

'They're here,' she said, 'I've got them.'

She walked to the house and Parker followed her.

In the living-room the big painting of Julia Naundorff looked down from the wall. It still seemed out of place.

Julia's papers were in a downstairs room that had been an office when the place belonged to a big farmer who had a large staff and many men to pay wages to. There were framed photographs on the wall of Ann as a child against the background of a fine-looking big house. Most of the photographs had Ann with horses or dogs. A man and woman appeared in some of them.

'My mother and father, at home in Pennsylvania,' she said, having caught Parker sneaking looks at them. He had thought that his great height would have concealed his eye line.

There were no photos of Kimberly and Julia.

Parker was going to ask about Kimberly. He wanted to know why Ann hadn't invited her to stay. He didn't know how to go about asking a question like that.

Ann got the papers out. 'Do you want to take these along or will you read them here?' she asked.

Parker thought he could get through them there, he was a lawyer, he could shift through legal papers as easily as reading a newspaper.

Ann left him and he sat quite still for an hour and a half carefully going through that part of Julia Naundorff's life that had little to do with the baffled blonde that appeared on the screen, expect that it showed the sometimes rather wonderful financial rewards she got for looking dumb and sexy in front of the cameras.

There was much property bought and sold. She owned none of it at the time of her death, and the money seemed to have vanished. A tax accountant would have grown suspicious, thinking the money was hidden away some-where. She had paid off a mortgage on Ann's house, but she was broke, at least broke compared to the millions she had once possessed. She had $10,000 in one account and $143,000 in another. If Parker had that, he would con-sider himself not doing too bad. In fact he would have thought he was very well off. He thought Spendlove would also think it riches. It was enough money for someone like Spendlove to kill for, Parker thought.

Julia owned the farm, a car, jewellery, clothes and the

antique silver, also the rights on several movie scripts and a novel that could possibly be made into a picture. Parker had never heard of the novel or its author. He recognised a name on one of the movie scripts. It was Jack Coolidge. Julia Naundorff had bought the rights of a script of his.

Parker sat at the desk and wondered if Julia Naundorff owning the rights to someone's screenplay was reason enough for that someone to kill her. He was at a loss, just as he was lost when it came to thinking that dying with $153,000 in cash in the bank was dying broke. Still, Spendlove must have thought he was in for millions, maybe $153,000 did look like a handful of change when you looked at it that way. Parker thought it was certainly enough money for Kimberly Naundorff to contest the will.

The room he was in was pleasant, very quiet, with the sunlight coming through the window and lighting the white painted sill and then creating comfortable-looking shadows behind the big old-fashioned furniture. Parker thought maybe he should go along with Davy Shea and let Dean Judd take the rap. It would be nice to stop thinking about murder.

He glanced round the room. The wallpaper was old. In places it had light patches and nail holes where pictures had been. There were many light patches. He opened the desk drawers to see if the pictures had been put there.

There were no pictures in the desk.

He heard footsteps coming along the hall and quickly closed the drawer. He looked at the wall where a photo of Ann, holding a horse in front of the house in Pennsylvania, looked at him.

'I haven't got a chance there,' he said to himself.

Ann came into the room. 'Have you found anything?' she asked.

'Nothing much.'

'I suppose you're surprised by what little money she had. Everyone seems more surprised by that than the fact that she was murdered. But they wouldn't be surprised if they knew her. If they really knew her, they'd know she could never hold on to money.'

'You know,' Parker said, 'it seems like a lot of money to me.'

'To me too,' she said, 'but when you remember the money Julia used to make . . . '

She let this idea hang about in the air for a moment and then she said, 'Would you like something to drink? I've got some more of that lemonade.'

Parker felt like a hired man who was being offered refreshment. He didn't know if it was Ann's tone or something in himself that made him think this. Probably both, he thought.

'No thanks,' he said, 'I have to go.'

'Oh,' she said. She sounded disappointed. 'Are you off to chase after the runaway man?'

'I guess I'll have some of that lemonade,' he said.

'Well, come on,' she said.

He followed her through dusty but tasteful rooms, looking at her long legs and the curve of her backside. He forgot Jack Coolidge's movie script that might be a tremendous leap in the investigation.

In the kitchen the Staffordshire bull terrier was chewing something in a corner and looked up at them with only momentary interest.

'Moll,' Ann said, 'what's that?' She reached down and took a sock from the dog. 'I suppose it's beyond repair,' she said. She returned it to the dog, but the dog was no longer interested. The sock, bright red with a black diamond pattern, lay unmolested.

Parker said, 'Did your sister ever mention a movie script she'd bought?'

'You mean the one she bought from Jack Coolidge?'

Parker was surprised that she knew, but then he thought, of course she'd have read the papers.

'I don't remember,' she said. 'She might have said something. When she said she wasn't going to do any more

178

movies she might have said something about the scripts she'd been offered.'

'This was one she bought,' Parker said. 'She must have liked it and considered doing it.'

'Maybe she only liked Jack Coolidge. He *is* good-looking.'

Parker had the usual male difficulty knowing what a woman considered good-looking in a man; and Ann had seen Jack only once, under trying circumstances, with her sister's body lying on the boatdock. It seemed incredible that she would have taken in Coolidge's looks in a gruesome situation like that, but then, even with having just found Billy Zoots with his throat cut, Parker had taken in Ann's long legs getting out of the jeep; and he had looked at Ann with Julia dead on the boatdock. He had thought that was only his crude Liberty Street background, and being male, but evidently a woman like Ann could also be distracted in the same way by a good-looking man.

She gave him a glass of lemonade. He stood like the hired man who is not asked to sit down, but she stood close to him. The dark brown eyes of the Staffordshire bull terrier seated on the floor were on them as if she could sense an atmosphere.

'I saw you the other night,' Parker said. 'At the Lake House.'

'Oh, yes, Whitey took me out to dinner.'

Whitey Gotton was another crude male, from a no more classy background than Parker himself. But this evidently didn't put her off.

'There's nothing between Whitey and me,' she said. She still stood close to him.

Parker didn't know what to say.

'I must go,' he said.

Ann laughed. Parker glanced about, as if the dog might have done something amusing with the sock, but he knew why Ann had laughed.

She took his glass and put it on the table.

'Now Moll,' she said to the dog, 'don't do that.' Moll was pulling at the laces of a boot. Ann, hardly turning to look at Parker, said, 'Come back sometime when you're not being a detective.'

'That'd be nice,' Parker said.

He drove down the bumpy drive and out of Old Compton to Brown's Ferry to cross the lake.

There were tourists up and about, and he had to wait some time for a place on the car ferry to carry him across the water to the Lake House to see Jack Coolidge.

The tourists were talking of Julia Naundorff's murder. He heard one of them say, 'He's the sheriff, over there, the tall one.'

Parker saw himself being pointed at. He thought he heard laughter, but he might be imagining it.

'They've got someone for it,' one of the passengers said, 'they've caught the guy who killed them all, but then they let him escape.'

42

He came up the steps to the Lake House and at the reception desk he was about to ask for Jack Coolidge when someone said, 'It's Boomer Daniels. Hello, Boomer, come and have a drink.'

He turned to see Sally Sallas sitting in the lobby. He was wearing a plaid shirt, a fishing vest, chinos, and heavy-duty shoes, all brand new.

'I've been out fishing,' he said. 'The sun came out, the lake got too crowded and noisy and, thank God, I was able to escape. What'll you have?'

He got to his feet. He didn't come up very far on Parker, but he made up for it by being much wider.

'Jack's in the bar getting us drinks. Tell me what you want.'

'I guess I'm not supposed to drink,' Parker said.

'You mean on duty? You're on duty now? Are you going to arrest someone else? I thought you'd got the perp, but he escaped?'

'I don't know,' Parker said, 'maybe later I might arrest someone else.'

'If the mood strikes you,' Sallas said.

Parker sat down. He said, 'I suppose you must think us a pack of hicks, in a backwoods place like this.'

'What you mean? Are you going to arrest me for murder? The yokel sheriff outsmarting the city slicker?'

Parker could see Sallas didn't take himself seriously as a suspect.

'No,' Parker said, 'at least I don't think I'll arrest you, not right now anyway.'

Jack Coolidge came in from the bar. He was dressed for fishing like Sally Sallas but his clothes weren't new.

Sallas said, 'It's all right, Jack, Boomer isn't going to arrest you. At least not right now.'

Parker didn't say anything.

'God, this place is the back of beyond,' Sallas said. 'They don't got nothing here but murders.'

Coolidge said, 'They've got a theatre.'

'Oh, sure,' Sallas said, 'in the summer they've got a theatre so the tourists can pretend they're not far from culture after a day out in the great outdoors getting eaten by bugs.'

'It's not bad,' Coolidge said, 'the theatre here is pretty good.'

'Who you kidding?' Sallas said. 'You'd go bananas living in a place like this. You left that hick town you were born in because you were dying there and now you're being nostalgic, or only polite.'

Coolidge said to Parker, 'Don't listen to him. This place

is just fine. Sal wouldn't know culture if it bit him on the leg.'

Parker said, 'Julia Naundorff bought a movie script of yours.'

Sallas said, 'I knew it. He's going to arrest us. Or at least he's going to arrest you, Jack. Is that right, Boomer?'

'I'm going to have to arrest someone pretty soon,' Parker said.

'But you've already got the guy.'

'I didn't get him. That was another cop who got him.'

'So,' Sallas said, 'in this town each cop goes out and arrests his own favourite suspect and then what do you do, flip a coin? Arrest that loony reincarnation guy. He'd be a popular choice. Jack could write a movie about it. We'd get a classy English sir to play him. You want to know about that script Julia bought off Jack? I'll tell you about that script. She went off her head, that's what she did. She thought since no one wanted to see her in a movie any more, she'd become a producer. Can you imagine that? A dumb bitch like that being a producer of motion pictures?'

Sallas waited for this to sink in. Then he said:

'I told her she was crazy, throwing away what little money she had left, but because she'd made it big in one line of work, she thought she could make it in another. I told her it didn't work that way, but she wouldn't listen. That's all there is to that. We came up here like we said, to get her to play a small part in another movie Jack is writing. That other script that she owned? We weren't thinking about that. Let her keep it. No offence meant, Jack, but it wasn't one of your best.'

'I liked it,' Coolidge said.

'Of course you did or you wouldn't have written it. But it wasn't something you'd kill for. I mean, it wasn't a script you'd come up here and murder Julia in order to get it away from her. That, I think, is the point in question. That is what Boomer is trying to clear up. Isn't that right, chief?'

Parker said, 'I was wondering what a still good-looking woman like Julia Naundorff was doing, leaving the life she led in Los Angeles to come here.'

Sallas said, 'You should ask the sister. She'd be the one who'd know why Julia came here. But I can see you're thinking of something more dramatic, of a woman on the run from the Mob on account of she stole the money from a drug deal. Isn't that right?'

'I've got a sergeant who likes that idea,' Parker said.

'Sure he does,' Sallas said. 'What hick cop wouldn't? It'd make his little life here in the boondocks more like something in the movies. A man who can have something in his life like a scene out of the movies hasn't lived in vain. Jesus, Jack,' he said to Coolidge, 'you got a lot to answer for, that crap you and the rest of 'em write for the pictures.'

43

When Parker came down the front steps of the Lake House he saw Phyllis Skypeck on the boatdock. He walked down to her.

'Parker,' she said, 'come for a ride.'

She stepped into a small boat. There was an outboard motor attached to it. She reached out and held on to the dock, while Parker climbed down into the boat.

She had her fishing rod and tackle box in the boat. Phyllis pulled the cord on the outboard several times and the motor wouldn't start.

She gripped the wooden handle to pull the cord again. The cord passed through the handle and was tied into a knot. It was a fancy knot.

'Whose boat is this?' Parker asked.

'It's mine,' she said, 'but this damned motor is Whitey Gotton's.'

She pulled again and the motor started.

She sat down in the stern facing him. 'I thought I'd like to go for a little ride. After fishing this morning in the same spot I thought I'd like to move about a bit. I saw you in the Lake House talking to those two men. They were scared of you.'

That's a good one, Parker thought. It showed that people didn't always know what they were looking at and made up what they wanted to be seeing.

Phyllis steered the boat to cross the lake at its narrowest part, where the car ferry was busy carrying tourists, and then she turned and skimmed along the shore with a scenic view of open fields and mountains in the distance. After a while she throttled back and they crawled along. Parker didn't look at the shore and the beautiful scenery. He was looking at the knot.

He looked away.

It was a heavenly morning without a breath of wind. A herd of black and white Friesian cows was grazing close to the shore. First one, then two, then four others came slowly down to the water's edge. One cow got down the bank into the water and stood looking aimlessly about, then with some difficulty climbed up the bank back into the pasture.

Across the lake came the faint sound of an airplane engine. Parker, turning to look, saw a seaplane taxiing to take off, sending up much spray. Close by the boat a fish jumped and made a smacking noise as it returned to the water, a lazy summer sound.

He looked at Phyllis. Her finger nails had bright red polish. She saw what he was looking at. She held a hand up, showing him the nail varnish.

'A trifle overdone,' she said. 'I went out on the hunt last night. Then this morning I was in too much of a hurry to take it off.' She laughed. 'God,' she said, 'you should see your face. I'm sorry if you disapprove.'

She was still keeping close to the shore. The boat sent

waves against the bank, disturbing a small water bird that came out of the reeds.

'I'd better pull away from the shore,' Phyllis said. 'I'm disturbing that fisherman. Jesus, it's my father. He shouldn't be fishing, he should be working, but so should I.'

Parker couldn't see anyone.

'Where?' he said.

'There,' Phyllis said.

She pointed to the bank where tall bushes came down to the water. What Parker thought was a tall, slender reed moved and he saw it was a fishing rod. Fred Skypeck was hidden in the thicket. His head and then his arm appeared holding the rod.

Skypeck saw his daughter. He seemed surprised to see Parker with her.

'Are you being arrested?' he called.

She turned the boat out into the middle of the lake.

'He'll think I'm after you now, Parker,' she said. 'He's worried about me chasing after men. How about if I did chase after you? Would you run? Are you too busy being chased by Ann West to bother with a girl with dirty hair and last night's nail polish on her hands? Ann West is one of those lucky creatures who doesn't need make-up.'

She was headed back to the Lake House Hotel dock. Parker could see Sally Sallas and Jack Coolidge sitting on the hotel porch.

She pulled into the dock and Parker got out.

He scarcely noticed her take the boat back into the middle of the lake. He went home to make some telephone calls.

44

Parker drove to Liberty Street where he found Maria Esperanza in the ground floor rooms of the late Elroy Green. She still couldn't remember what was strange about the man she saw in the backyard on the day of the murder.

'Never mind,' Parker said, 'I've something else I want you to do.'

When he left her, he went back to the station. Davy Shea and Georgie Stover were there.

'Listen,' Parker said, 'there's a job I want you to do. Get Ed Ross and Bob Vanderland.'

'What's up?' Davy said.

When Parker told him Davy said, 'What the hell's the point of this? We've got a dangerous man on the run. He's our first priority.'

Parker said, 'Judd didn't do it.'

'I suppose you know who did?' Davy said.

'That's right,' Parker said. 'I do.'

Davy glanced at Georgie to see if he also thought Parker was crazy.

'Well,' Davy said when Parker didn't say anything else, 'who did it?'

'I'm not telling you,' Parker said, 'you couldn't keep your mouth shut if I did.'

'Thanks,' Davy said, 'but I still say we've got our man.'

Georgie came up to Parker and said, 'Are you sure about bringing Vanderland along?'

'We may need him,' Parker said.

'I'm not sure about him,' Georgie said.

Parker knew that Georgie didn't like the rich kid.

'He's trouble,' Georgie said, 'he wants to shoot someone.'

He glanced at Davy and Parker knew he wanted to say that Vanderland wanted to shoot someone as badly as Davy did, but of course he couldn't say it.

'I know,' Parker said, 'but what the hell can we do? We're stuck with him.'

Parker left the station and drove the six miles to Holford. The city was unpleasant in the windless heat. The bright sun showed how rundown the old milltown had become.

He parked the DeSoto in a side street by the office of the *Holford Transcript*. The battered car looked right at home in the grimy street.

He found young Ed Steiger in the *Transcript*.

'You're really going to do that?' the reporter said when Parker told him what he had come for.

'That's right,' Parker said.

'It sounds crazy to me,' Steiger said, 'but it's a good story.'

It was also dangerous, but Parker didn't tell the reporter that.

He drove home thinking that Georgie Stover was probably right about Bob Vanderland, but he needed the extra man, however trigger-happy he might be.

He was sitting on his porch considering this when Spa Johnson came up the street carrying a copy of the *Transcript*. Spa came up on the porch and sat down making himself right at home on the glider.

'How about this?' he said. 'This some more of your masterful work, Boomer?'

It was the story Parker had given Ed Steiger. The famous Boston hypnotist, H. P. Spendlove, was going to put Maria Esperanza into a trance to get her to remember the man she had seen at the scene of Elroy Green's murder.

Spa said, 'When she's under a hypnotic spell and identifies the man in the backyard, will that stand up in court?'

Parker didn't say anything.

Spa said, 'I don't think that would be admissible evidence.'

After a little while Spa left and Parker continued to sit on the porch until it began to grow dark.

45

The window overlooking the backyard was open. There was a full moon but the sky was filled with clouds and the effect was as though a light was switched on and off as they moved across the moon.

Parker was in the room that had been Elroy Green's. Maria Esperanza sat on the bed. The only movement in the room was the stirring of the curtains at the window. The clairvoyant remained still and silent, her eyes on the window.

Parker sat hidden in a corner. His eyes were also on the window. When the breeze moved the curtain he could see out into the backyard. In the moonlight the uncut grass and the grapevine that grew over the rickety fence blocking off the alley had the look of something in the tropics.

He had been here for some time now and he had begun to think that the trap he had set was a foolish business. Ed Ross was on guard, hidden outside in the street at the front of the house, but if Ross was getting bored, as bored as Parker was, he would get careless and show himself. Not that Parker thought the killer would walk up to the front door. He would come the back way if he came, using the cover of the dark alley and the overgrown backyard to enter Maria Esperanza's room by the window. It was the way the killer came to get Elroy Green and Parker was sure he'd come that way again.

Davy Shea, Georgie Stover and Bob Vanderland were hidden at various points in the back alley. They were to let the killer through. Parker would need the evidence of an actual attack to get a conviction in court. 'That's comic-book stuff,' he said to himself now, waiting in the dark room. Then he thought, no, it's not. It's a stake-out, an accepted practice, police procedure. The only thing is, I've never done it before.

What he hadn't realised was that it took so long and was painful as well as boring, waiting crouched down in the dark.

'I could have got it all wrong,' he said to himself.

He wanted to whisper to Maria Esperanza, ask her how she was doing, staked out like a tethered goat waiting for the tiger. When the breeze blew the curtain aside he could see her handsome face in the moonlight only two feet away from where he crouched on the floor. He could hear her breathing. 'She's agitated, but at least she's not bored,' Parker thought, 'a woman waiting for someone to come in and try to strangle her like he strangled Elroy Green or cut her throat like Billy Zoots is not going to be bored.'

Parker made an effort to imagine the scene outside. He knew the back alley very well. He'd known it when he was a kid. He'd played in it, and he'd walked down it plenty of times in the dark.

'Will he come?' Maria Esperanza whispered.

She didn't turn her head to look at Parker. She kept staring at the window, whispering to him out of the side of her mouth.

'I don't know,' Parker whispered back.

He also kept his eyes on the window. He thought of Davy and the others fidgeting in their hiding places in the alley. The way things were going, Bob Vanderland would probably pull his gun out and shoot himself in the leg. It would be almost worth it if Vanderland shot himself. It'd teach him what guns were all about.

Parker had a gun. The old Smith and Wesson .38 was tucked into the waistband of his trousers.

The breeze was getting up. The window curtain flapped

against the wall and outside the wind blew the branches of a tree against the side of the house.

And there was another noise.

'What's that?' he asked.

'The wind,' she said.

'No, the other noise?'

There was the creak of footsteps on the floor in the room above them.

Maria said, 'That's Estelle.'

Parker hadn't told Estelle Ritter he was coming to Liberty Street. She wouldn't have been able to keep her mouth shut about it. Also she would have been a nervous wreck. He thought she'd be well out of it up on the top floor.

'She doesn't live up there,' Parker said.

'She does now,' Maria Esperanza said, 'she moved into my old room on account of her legs.'

'Jesus,' Parker said, 'I never thought of that.'

He wasn't whispering although he was speaking more to himself than to Maria.

'They don't know you've moved,' he said. 'They think that's you up there. I've got to get up there. Listen, take the gun in case I'm wrong. If anyone comes in, shoot them.'

They could hear the footsteps upstairs clearly now. More than footsteps. There was a struggle going on in the room directly above.

Parker ran up the stairs. The door to Estelle's room was locked. If he'd had the gun he could have shot it open.

He could hear furniture going over in the room, then he threw himself against the door. He heard the fighting inside stop. He stood back and lifted his right leg and slammed his foot against the lock. The door flew open.

He could see Estelle lying on the floor. She didn't move. There was someone else moving about.

'Stay where you are. It's all over,' he said. 'There's police all around outside.'

190

The figure paused for a moment, a black figure in the window. Then stepped out onto the fire escape.

'Davy,' Parker called out, 'she's coming through the backyard.'

He climbed out of the window after her, but when he looked down she wasn't there.

Then he saw the opened window to Maria Esperanza's room. He climbed through. They were fighting on the floor. He could see the two yellow-haired heads, but he couldn't tell which was which.

Parker grabbed Ann West, pulling her off the floor, holding her arms behind her.

'Where's the gun?' he asked.

'I've got it,' Maria Esperanza said. 'When I saw her I held it up but I couldn't fire it.'

Outside the gunfire was still going on.

A window in the house next door opened.

'What the hell's going on out there?' a voice asked.

'It's all right, lady,' Davy, in the backyard, said.

'What's happening in the alley?' Parker shouted.

Davy's face appeared at the window.

He said, 'I guess Georgie and Vanderland have found someone.'

Then he peered in the room.

'Who's that?' he asked. 'It's her. I never thought it would be her.'

The woman next door shouted down from the upstairs window. 'Hey, you,' she said to Davy, 'that gunfire doesn't sound all right to me.'

'Come in here,' Parker said to Davy.

Davy climbed through the window. He had his gun drawn.

'Hold her,' Parker said. 'I've got to go upstairs to see if Estelle's all right.'

'I did first aid,' Maria Esperanza said, 'I'll come.'

Parker ran up the stairs. 'It's my fault,' he said to

himself, 'I've killed her as sure as if I strangled her myself.'

Estelle was still lying on the floor. He expected to see a cord round her neck, but there was no cord.

Maria Esperanza came in after him and knelt beside the body.

'She's alive,' she said.

Estelle's eyes opened.

'The noise out there,' she said, 'that's Blanche Laporte shouting. But who's doing all the shooting?'

'You OK?' Parker asked.

'What a question,' Estelle said. 'I'm moving back to the top floor, the lazy bastards don't climb up after you there.'

'I'll stay with her,' Maria Esperanza said.

Parker went back downstairs.

'Who's that in the alley?' Davy said. 'Is it Whitey?'

'It's not Whitey,' Parker said.

'It has to be,' Davy said. 'Who else can it be?'

'I'm afraid it's someone else,' Parker said.

'You're crazy,' Davy said.

Ann stood silent with Davy holding her.

There was the sound of running footsteps in the back-yard.

'It's OK,' Georgie shouted, 'we got him.'

'Let's go,' Parker said to Ann.

They went out the backdoor and across the yard and through a gate in the fence to the alley and she still didn't say anything.

Georgie said, 'I couldn't see who it was. It's so dark here. We heard someone shouting in the house and Vanderland fired and whoever it was in the car in the alley shot back and then we fired.'

Vanderland came out of the shadows. He had a gun in his hand. They could see a big smile on his college-boy face. 'I got him,' he said. 'He's dead.'

Ann spoke now. 'You bastards,' she said, 'you goddam sons of bitches.'

Davy bent over and looked into the car. 'Jesus, Boomer,' he said, 'how can this be?'

Spa Johnson was slumped dead behind the wheel.

46

In the morning Parker made some telephone calls from home and then he went to the station where he learned that the police in Clairmont, New Hampshire had picked up Dean Judd.

'That clears it up,' Davy said.

'I don't know if it does,' Parker said. It was just before lunchtime and he said, 'I'm going to the College Inn. You'd better come with me.'

'What for?' Davy asked.

'We'll have to see,' Parker said.

At the College Inn, H. P. Spendlove, looking sharp but with his glasses still held together by tape, was sitting on a sofa next to Maria Esperanza. They were holding hands and looked like $153,000 wasn't getting in the way of a reconciliation.

Spendlove was buying drinks but Parker wasn't having any. He didn't feel like celebrating either Spa's death or Ann West being locked up for murder.

'What's going on, Boomer?' Davy asked.

He was uncomfortable being with people he had been busy accusing of murder only the day before yesterday.

'There's someone else we've got to arrest,' Parker said.

Phyllis came into the lounge. She said she'd come to see the son of a couple staying in the hotel. The kid had broken out in spots. It was measles.

Sally Sallas and Jack Coolidge wandered in. Sallas said they had come because Coolidge, being a scriptwriter, was nosey and wanted to find out what happened and they had told them at the station where Parker was.

Kimberly Naundorff was waiting on in the lounge, but she wasn't happy. She'd lost her big blonde glow.

'So,' Sallas said, 'how'd you figure it, Boomer?'

He was making himself at home, taking a seat by the Spendloves as if he were the father of the bride. 'Sit down,' he said to Parker, 'tell us how you figured it. Jack is keen to know, aren't you, Jack?'

Parker glanced at Coolidge. He was sitting next to Phyllis and he didn't seem all that much interested in crime.

Then Whitey Gotton walked in, looking around as if expecting someone. He saw Phyllis and walked over to her.

'Hi,' he said, and sat down next to her.

'What I don't know,' Sallas said, 'is how Julia got murdered with me and Jack there all the time in the boat and Jack looking at her and not seeing anything.'

Parker said, 'It was there all the time for me to see, but I was too thick to see it. The thing is, that's a quiet cove where Ann's house is, but it's not good fishing, if you hadn't been from out of town, you'd have known that. Ann could normally count on no one being there, but just in case she had to get her sister into the water so anyone looking would think it was an accidental drowning.'

'But how did Julia get into the water?' Sallas asked.

'What killed her was something Coolidge couldn't see, even though he was looking at her,' Parker said.

'What couldn't I see?' Coolidge said.

'Your boat was a good distance away and there was the morning haze,' Parker said. 'What you couldn't see was the fishing line. Later on I was on the shore and I could see you, but I couldn't see your lines when you cast.'

'A fishing line?' Kimberly said. She sat down suddenly at the table.

'That's right,' Parker said, 'with a heavy weight attached to it.'

'That could knock her out,' Whitey Gotton said, 'hitting her in the right place. In fact it could kill her.'

'It did,' Parker said, 'they were going to drown her once she was in the water, but it hit her harder than they thought it would. They were unlucky there. Phyllis was able to tell us that Julia hadn't drowned, that she was dead from a blow on the temple before she hit the water. We knew it was murder then.'

'How'd you come up with a man with a fishing rod?' Coolidge said.

'You said something that led me to it,' Parker said. 'When you were describing the scene to me, you said you saw the bushes moving in the breeze, but there was no wind that morning. It was dead calm. Later on I was out in a boat with Phyllis. Her father was fishing, but he was hidden in the reeds on the bank. I saw his rod moving and I mistook it for a reed waving in the wind.'

Parker said to Whitey, 'I thought of you. You were the champion caster. You had known Julia Naundorff in Los Angeles when you were playing ball there. But I knew from Phyllis that that blown-out shoulder of yours was getting worse.'

'That's a fact,' Whitey said. 'I severed a group of capsule ligaments and they never healed. I had a two-hour operation on my shoulder. An orthopaedist did it. A *distinguished* orthopaedist, but it was never any good any more. I couldn't pitch a ball and now I'm getting so I can't cast a line.'

'You weren't the only expert,' Parker said. 'Almost every kid on the lake is pretty damn good at casting. Good enough anyway for what Ann wanted done.'

'She didn't do it herself?' Kimberly said.

She stared at Parker, eager to know who killed her famous daughter.

Parker said, 'It was Ann's idea, but she didn't do it. Spa was the fisherman in the bushes. His brother Edgar told me he was always taking time off school to go fishing. He was quite a champion at it, but it didn't fit in with his cool image, so he stopped.'

'But he was holding up Gleason's liquor store,' Phyllis said.

Parker saw she was worried that he had got it wrong and Spa was an innocent victim of trigger-happy police.

'Gleason's Liquor Mart isn't far from Ann's place in Old Compton. Spa had plenty of time to get there. He was delayed by Billy Zoots's witnessing him. That was something he and Ann hadn't planned on. But even so, he could get to Gleason's and pretend to be robbing it. He even had time to dry off, all but his shoes. They were still wet. It was clever going in pretending to be a Puerto Rican and doing it so badly and then stopping everything to look at a movie star. It was so half-ass nobody would question it. I didn't. I felt sorry for him. I took him to be just what he wanted me to, which was a crazy kid who didn't know what he was doing. But then I met his brother and I found out that Spa wasn't like that. He was middle class, and not a kid like I thought, but a man of twenty-five. Even his name wasn't right. He was Bob Johnson, he'd only just started calling himself Spa. It's West Indian slang, it fit in with the part he was playing.'

'OK,' Phyllis said, 'but people saw Julia Naundorff driving round North Holford town centre.'

'They saw a blonde in Julia Naundorff's car, a car with California plates. They made the assumption.'

'What was the motive behind all this?' Phyllis asked.

Sallas said, 'Is there a motive? There wasn't any real money. Spendlove gets what there is.'

'Just a minute,' Whitey said, 'you mean she let me come down there with my nieces to have them discover the body? It gave those kids nightmares for a week. They're still having them.'

'I'm afraid she wasn't as nice as any of us thought,' Parker said. 'And when Elroy Green was strangled she tied the cord with a fancy knot like you use, Whitey. Spa even pointed out that fancy knot to me. They wanted to drop you in it.'

'What about me?' Spendlove said. 'Look what she tried to do to me.'

'Yes,' Parker said, 'you were the other patsy. They didn't mind us thinking Whitey had done it, but you were the main fall guy. It was Ann, not Julia, who telephoned you and asked you to come to the house. If the police were going to get suspicious, she wanted them to have someone other than herself to be suspicious about. You were perfect, being the one Julia was leaving her money to, but it got complicated when Billy Zoots and Elroy Green came to rob the house and Zoots saw Spa killing Julia. Spa had to kill him. Spa knew Zoots worked with Elroy Green and he couldn't take a chance on Elroy having seen him so he had to be killed too. But he didn't kill Green, Ann did that. What was strange about the man Maria Esperanza saw in the backyard at Liberty Street was that it was a woman dressed as a man.'

'I glanced out the window and I saw someone there,' Maria Esperanza said. 'They had clothes like yours, Archie. I thought it was you spying on me, but then I saw it wasn't you. But I didn't realise right away that it was a woman.'

'But what was the motive?' Phyllis asked again. 'There doesn't seem to be a motive.'

'That bothered me for a long time,' Parker said. 'I kept thinking money had to be behind it, that's why I thought it must have been Mr Spendlove or possibly some business arrangement between Sal Sallas and Jack Coolidge. But there wasn't anything. I began to think her friendship with the Mob had something to do with it. That would have been bad, it would have been too big for us hick cops to tackle. Then we thought we might be up against a madman killing people with yellow hair. I almost started believing that. I also thought for a time it might have been Dick Doyle. He had a motive for killing Julia, but he had an alibi for the time of her death. But Dick gave me something that put me on to a possible motive. But then I got the idea that Ann had a very settled life and suddenly it was getting disrupted. Julia had bailed Ann out when the farm had run into trouble and Ann had to take out a mortgage which she couldn't repay. Julia bought the house and farm from her. Ann owed her a big favour, but Julia moving in to live was too much for her. When I saw Ann at her house, and then bringing the hay in, I could see how happy she was even if the work was hard. People don't just kill for money, they'll also do it to protect their way of life, and there was always the danger that Julia might sell the house and land. Then,' Parker said, 'when I connected Spa to Ann there was something else giving a pretty good motive.'

Kimberly said, 'What do you mean, *connected*?'

'Well,' Parker said, 'Spa was good-looking, a handsome guy. I saw him at Ann's house and he made up an excuse for being there and I believed him. But then I saw her dog playing with a sock in the kitchen. It was a man's sock and there weren't supposed to be any men in the house. It was a bright red sock. I'd seen it on Spa. It was the kind Spa wore when he was playing the sharp guy from the streets.'

'They were lovers, Ann and that guy?' Whitey said. 'I knew there must be someone else, but I never thought.'

Phyllis said, 'You've forgotten something, Parker. If Ann was there when Julia went into the water, who was driving around town pretending to be Julia?'

'That confused me,' Parker said, 'I thought it must be her. When I met her for the first time that morning, she was wearing lots of mascara and lipstick and had bright red nail polish. She never wore make-up like that again, even when she was being taken out to dinner by Whitey at the Lake House. But her alibi was solid. She'd been seen shopping when Julia was driving round North Holford. Then I realised what had happened. Ann had taken Julia's car with the California plates and driven out and met up with someone and that person took over the role of Julia. Ann got out of her movie star clothes and back into a T-shirt and shorts, but she didn't have time to remove the make-up.'

'And who was it who pretended she was Julia?' Sallas asked.

'The other sister,' Parker said.

'Who's the other sister?' Sallas said. 'I never heard Julia mention her.'

'She wouldn't. She was nobody important, just an older sister who Julia never helped out, even when she was making a lot of money.'

'There was never another sister,' Kimberly said, 'and I ought to know.'

Parker looked at her, but he didn't speak to her.

He said to Sallas, 'When I was in Ann's house reading through Julia's papers I saw the wallpaper was a different colour where pictures had been. There were many framed family photographs on the walls and there were blank spaces and nail holes where others had been. That seemed strange to me. I thought they must have been photos of Julia and that Ann had taken them down because she didn't want to be reminded of her murdered stepsister, but there was a large picture of Julia in the living-room and that hadn't been removed. I began to think that Ann was hiding something from her past. I telephoned Pennsylvania to find out about the woman Ann's father had married, and then I called Mississippi and I found that her mother was dead.'

'That's right,' Sallas said, 'Julia said her mother was dead, but I thought she was being a bitch and meant she was dead to her.'

'She was a bitch,' Kimberly said. 'I took care of mama all the time she was ill. I wrote to Julia but she never answered. How'd you get on to me?' she asked Parker.

'I believed the story of you being the child bride,' Parker

said, 'but there was something about your acting the big dumb Southern blonde that didn't ring true, any more than Bob Johnson's performance as Spa did.'

'And I thought you were just a long streak of lonesome,' Kimberly said.

No one seemed to have anything else to say. Parker and Davy took Kimberly to the station.

'I didn't tell them anything,' Ann said to her.

'I know you didn't, honey,' Kimberly said.

Then Parker and Davy drove out to the house in Old Compton to find the missing photographs.

They weren't in the desk and they searched for a long time before they found them in the back of a kitchen cupboard.

There were photos of Ann and Kimberly with their arms round each other looking like great pals in spite of the age difference. In another photo they were with the mother and she looked the sort of homey woman a man might think would make a good wife and stepmother. There were photos of Julia, too, and even as a kid she didn't look very pleasant.

They came out of the house and one of the men who worked on the farm came up to them.

'Boomer,' he said, 'I got trouble at home. My wife's got cats and she don't like that dog of Ann's. Will you take it off my hands?'

Parker said he would.

'That'll be good for you,' Davy said.

He meant that it would give Parker something to love, but he didn't say it. It would have sounded too sad.